About the Author

David has seen and experienced life in many sectors of the world. Born in Kenya (then East Africa) he was educated there and in Yorkshire. There he developed many hobbies, including wildlife and many sports. He graduated from the veterinary college, London, before working in Australia.

Back to the UK he worked for an international drug company developing medicines and vaccines.

Born with an interest in stories, books, literature, and writing led to his becoming an author after retirement.

He has now developed an abiding wish to advance inborn abilities to think out new stories; and to involve any reader interested in solving the Murder Mystery.

Particular fascination for detective fiction, by famous historians since years BC stimulated an insatiable desire to evolve a new prototype of modern detective. One who uses intellect and ingenuity to understand and unmask murderers who have so far eluded the police.

The Ikon Mythman Murder Mystery novels follow this desire as hopefully a successful author.

Ikon Mythman

---

2 + 2 M A Y B 5

AUSTIN MACAULEY PUBLISHERS™
LONDON · CAMBRIDGE · NEW YORK · SHARJAH

Copyright © Ikon Mythman 2023

The right of Ikon Mythman to be identified as author of this work has been asserted by the author in accordance with sections 77 and 78 of the Copyright, Designs and Patents Act 1988.

All rights reserved. No part of this publication may be reproduced, stored in a retrieval system, or transmitted in any form or by any means, electronic, mechanical, photocopying, recording, or otherwise, without the prior permission of the publishers.

Any person who commits any unauthorised act in relation to this publication may be liable to criminal prosecution and civil claims for damages.

This is a work of fiction. Names, characters, businesses, places, events, locales, and incidents are either the products of the author's imagination or used in a fictitious manner. Any resemblance to actual persons, living or dead, or actual events is purely coincidental.

A CIP catalogue record for this title is available from the British Library.

ISBN 9781398411470 (Paperback)
ISBN 9781398414280 (Hardback)
ISBN 9781398414297 (ePub e-book)

www.austinmacauley.com
First Published 2023
Austin Macauley Publishers Ltd
1 Canada Square
Canary Wharf
London
E14 5AA

Acknowledgements to Austin Macauley for helping new authors to find their way toward publication.

Chapter 1

Tom Friender, ex-police detective, strolled along the pathway just by the edge of a river-canal, his mind churning with a dilemma of *super* national importance. Unrelieved by the natural calm of the watery environment close around him, he inevitably asked himself, "What action should or could I take to protect, even save, the government in office and all persons involved with it?" Clearly, his thoughts insisted, identifying the perpetrator was absolutely vital; but why, when and how were each equally important to solving the giant enigma confronting him and his long-time colleague investigators in the force, more commonly called the Met.

The National Police had indubitably failed to identify and swiftly confine in prison the fiend who'd done the actual killing. *Murder* was too soft a tag to wrap around such a case; which was still baby-fresh to him. That fact hardened the special task the police had set him: to name and assist the Met in apprehension of the killer of such a senior minister in Parliament!

What next! And what, if any, help could he—a now-retired special investigator—call on right now? Had he, he questioned himself, enough criminal investigation experience as a chief inspector, particularly with murder, to provide the CID with answers they were hounding him for at this very moment?

Since the murder he had been assigned to unquestionably affected National Security, he was under serious obligation to resolve the mystery of 'Who Dunnit'. And, to make his task even more of a nightmare, he had to succeed in as short a time as humanly possible!

Parliament waited on no man, not even the PM!

Perplexed, Friender kicked a few loose pebbles from the canal footpath into the lazily moving water on his left to stir something into action. His searching thoughts however did not respond, other than to decide that he must return to the scene of crime in Westminster City, London. His body responded to that decision at once by turning to face the canal bridge over which he had strolled unhurriedly what seemed only minutes ago. He would return to his car a lot more swiftly to drive to the local railway station; *Action*, the sole response in his now switched-on mind to awaken all his investigatory senses.

The suburban train he had caught seemed to him to crawl into Waterloo Station, far too slow for an investigator, even be he private, seeking immediate answers. Opening the carriage door well before the slowing public transport had come to a halt between platforms, now *urgent* Tom left the train, heading for the underground to catch the tube to Waterloo.

On the way, his mind tried to unravel the curiosity of just how a senior MP could be murdered actually right in his work place; especially inside no less a place than the House of Commons! Where was security at the time?

'The House of Commons' part of the Palace of Westminster is a fascinating complex of buildings and structure, constructed over many centuries, including a fiery destruction. But this profile had no importance to him just at this moment—he had to get to the scene of murder quick as possible to further his investigation. He felt little reverence for the chambers and corridors, and statues, as he hurried along these towards his destination. A murder coated everything, including the location, in uncertainty and that to an investigator created a lack of any immediate real fascination or substance to the actual scene of crime!

"Oi!" bellowed a gruff voice behind him. "Where the hell d'you think you are? This's government special property belonging to Parliament. Show us your pass or else I'll 'ave to arrest yer!"

Pausing to turn, Friender was confronted by a big male in guard uniform. "I don't have any pass. I'm retired! But I'm here on *official* police business, investigating the murder of that MP that happened some days ago."

"Then you should ave a special pass you'd ave got from Scotland Yard, if yer who you say!" the loud-voiced guardian declared.

"Ah; you've every right to stop me, officer, BUT I really am working incognito for a special branch inspector to help with solving the murder case." He acted a big shrug of being blameless but the guard did not stop.

"OK, OK, officer! But before you push me out, any chance you'd assist me by explaining the security strategy for this House? I'd be very grateful for a general synopsis." He smiled an asking face.

"*Usual*; shifts and patrols of premises! What yer expect?" The officer maintained his dour response to the invasion of his duty patch in Parliament. "Quieter this minute 'cos the Houses are in recess."

The nosey inquisitor dropped silent for several minutes, mouth pursed and forehead furrowed in his attempt to decide the most profitable line of further questioning. His immediate problem of being challenged by authority was complicated by a real desire for a useful response from the policeman on guard. He did, after all, have a death-tainted episode in the history of the Palace to resolve mighty quick, no matter which line of research he chose to pursue.

Resolving 'Murder in Westminster', in no more vital a location than the House of Commons itself, was nothing less than a feat of very deliberate questioning of one and all, targeted at resolution of the foulest act of taking life he'd ever encountered as a senior investigator. So, was a speedy resolution of the case at all possible? He had to admit to an uncertain answer at this stage.

"I don't give tuppence who you are; either get out of 'ere or I'll be forced to arrest you." The pronouncement from the law was final in its gruff tone.

Friender decided it would be the most logical step for him to exit the House. It was thought-provoking in its mantle of history and current importance but a quick response to the indefensible situation seemed vital at this stage of the encounter.

"I appreciate your time in helping me," the investigator smiled a necessary class of smile for the occasion and headed for the exit.

Crossing the Central Lobby, where all corridors of the Historic Palace converged and which was topped by the Central Tower, he exited Parliament and stood for a while in one of the mighty pretty gardens to regain his thinking on the murder he was investigating. Buses and lorries roaring past along Millbank street did not deter him from his firm determination to 'get on with the investigation'.

Who and why would anyone murder as key a public figure as a senior MP, so to speak on his home ground, by precisely severing a major blood vessel in the man's neck? Had the poor victim been knocked out first; or tripped up and sat on, or just held tightly for long enough to execute the lethal cut? The resulting gush of bright red blood must have been nauseating to watch at real close quarters and the executer must have been ice-cold in their determination to end the MP's life!

From Westminster, he made his way to a temporary office that special branch had set up for him, but only while he investigated the murder of the centennial MP as he liked to envision it!

Thinking back in time, as he headed down an old painted corridor towards his room, the now departed MP had been charged with National Preservation as his special task; in addition to looking after his parliamentary constituency, which thrived not far outside the capital, London Westminster. No doubt a temporary minister had by now been appointed by the Speaker in Parliament to take over charge of the impending Preservation legislature. The ex-inspector's sharp brain analysed that such almost immediate answerability to the highest authority in the land would not be shouldered with much immediate elation! More importantly, the new man would probably prove of no immediate help to him, the private investigator, through lack of experience!

The moment he opened the door of his new office, Friender was confronted by the mass of mail, resembling a paper mill in abeyance that had already begun to cover his antique wooden desk. Every case of murder, or even assault-with-intent, that he had dealt with over twenty odd years had always involved endless postal communications! He'd not dealt with such a stark riddle as the murder of an MP before but he had no doubt whatsoever that this would result in even bigger packages of written communication from all manner of persons who had something to say or by-pen suggestions to make to him on how he should solve the mystery killing—once they found out he was on the case!

Although the exact location where the murdered MP's body had been found was well known, from HoC staff interviews and now the National Press, the Special Investigator himself had managed to collect only minimal data on the surroundings of the scene where the foul act had been committed. He knew full well from long experience that this data might be irrelevant as far as actual reasons for murder were concerned, but every detail was still, at this early stage, *vital*.

So, where to next? His intellect questioned. Would he progress quickest to identifying the unknown murderer by carefully studying all the mail or by revisiting the murder scene yet again, in case he had missed that vital clue, or—? Or *what*? A seasoned investigator never gave way to early confusion in seeking valid answers to a crime—so he would call on experience and go back to square one—revisit the scene of crime!

On his way walking back to the House of Commons, he busied his mind by mentally revisiting some of the facts that the Met had given him at his appointment interview with the senior inspector on the case. The MP had lived a straight-forward life dedicated to the public he encountered in his work. Most of that had been spent in or near London; the remainder out in the country along the River Thames and any linked-in canals. The victim had followed a business of legal aid, having qualified as a solicitor when he was young. His election as peoples' representative or MP had not gone un-hitched, but over the past two or three years there had been no public breaches of his voters' confidence in him.

So, for what possible logical reason had he been killed? The term 'Murder' eliminated the possibility of several killers to Friender. What as yet unidentified reasons lay behind the ending of an important public servant's life? Then, as always, the long-experienced investigator's querying mind kicked in. Was there any chance that the MP had somehow committed a suicide job? Then what in his recent life would have motivated such a dire and fatal action? Even with knife crime on the increase in most major cities, it took a really astonishing compulsion to murder an MP!

He reached the reported scene of death inside the HoC. He quickly took a restock of the close environment. Could it, in a strange fashion, have contributed to death? Or rather, did it shout clues as to the prime reason why the MP had been murdered exactly here? The investigator paused to assess just how far from a valid solution he had strayed, all in his haste to revisit the known facts of the case. There was not a shade of doubt that the MP had died right here; he could not possibly have walked or moved any distance with the fatal wound in his neck described by the police surgeon.

There had been no reports of death threats against the MP, Sir Peter Clark, in previous days or weeks or even months. He'd had no prime enemies that anyone who'd come forward to help the murder enquiry knew of. No person who his colleagues in the Met had questioned seemed pleased about the murder. So, what conclusion could he, retired investigator, draw? The sole, immediate decision he could make was to go back yet again to his desk up the road and to try his hardest to find useful leads amongst all the accumulated mail. Experience in the Met jogged his memory that the most unexpected clues often hatched from highly unexpected leads. Police urgency dictated this time that he had to explore even unexpected mental flashes of inspiration, no matter in which tangent they seemed to point. His overall cerebral urgency almost shouted, "The killer is still at large! They might strike again!"

Several days later, Friender felt satisfied he had identified more than a few fresh avenues worthy of investigation. He should visit the island up the Thames where the MP had a boat residence. Links between the MP's work platform and the House of Lords needed to be clarified. Any really close friends of the deceased must be talked to; in case they could give clues to the MP's world close around him. Local police and Parliamentary guardians must be fully interviewed. And anything else that cropped up during his investigations needed to be resolved, in case one or more could assist the investigator in his major quest—to positively identify the murderer as swiftly as possible!

Seated at the front window of the nearest cafe overlooking the street down from his office, Friender chatted amicably with the police inspector of the local force.

"Thanks again for meeting me here, Stan. Sorry once more to take up your time on today's duty schedule. You certainly don't need intruders like me in your zone of work! But who knows your station might just have the very clue I'm searching this site for!" He smiled knowingly at his police ex-companion.

"I doubt that, my friend! My colleagues have already submitted a very comprehensive report on the whole episode." Stan shrugged to emphasise his weariness with the whole event. "How come you got appointed to the investigation? You know the MP who was murdered, or something akin to that?"

The investigator knew from a vast experience of questioning that he simply must tread extremely carefully. To affront locally based contemporaries might prove irreparable—news and allegation rumours spread fast through police communication networks.

"Nothing very grand, Stan. I can assure you! Simply 'cos I wasn't too bungling in my early efforts to solve murder enquiries, the commissioner has developed a sort of respect for me and has often used me to solve difficult and unresolved enigmas of death that his police workers didn't seem able to."

"Blimey! So you're a clever dick! I just hope we can work together at my simple policing level!"

The ex-inspector wasted no further time satisfying the senior local man.

"That's why I'm on this murder case, Stan. Can you answer me this? Who was first to happen on the dead body?"

"Police. That's one of the patrolling HoC guards. And that's why the removal, identification and disposal of the body was done so quick!"

"Quite! Did the guard himself record anything he noted that was unexpected; given that discovery of a corpse in the House was remarkable in itself?" Friender pursed his lips.

"Since you asked, clever dick, apparently the dead MP was propped up as if he had been searched by someone."

Later, when the local policeman had long gone, the investigator finished his re-examination of the murder site and high-tailed it back to his office. His mood was not one of satisfaction but rather of the direct opposite, mixed with cerebral anger at his current inability to make any real progress. An outstanding Member of Parliament, recognised as skilful in handling and progressing vital new legislature, had been murdered by an unidentified assassin right there in the House of Commons—that's about as far as he'd got! For a retired senior inspector of the Met Special branch, that was what he'd call cheap policing, or even a waste of time and energy!

Inside Westminster Palace, in a room off the House of Commons Room, a meeting of the sub-committee on new Legislature was breaking up, business completed. A committee member slipped out to meet a lord in his office. "Have the police got any further with looking into Sir Peter Clark's death, my Lord?"

"In one, Andy, NO! And don't keep calling me 'my Lord'. We're old friends—so, no need!"

"OK, as you order." The parliamentary committee member shrugs. "Thought you'd now got a retired chief inspector from the Met Police to take over?"

"He's still under the current Met Police chief's command, not mine! If I get any progress report, I'll tell you so we can discuss how it might affect us in Parliament." The Lord's manner was cold and dismissive. So the MP left—hierarchy is everything in the two Houses. Also, neither parliamentarian was too obsessed with unearthing a killer right now.

In an entirely different corner of the Palace, two women were engaged in earnest conversation; their voices low and protective. "How we gonna save ourselves, Shirl? The more the bigwigs put two and two out to the House, we'll be good as cornered and shot! Can you keep the lid on amongst House colleagues till all goes quiet, in due time?"

Her bosom-buddy and long-term confidant grabbed her hand and squeezed it tight. "I can only do my damnedest, Pearl. But this 'ere is a very unified sort of society and legal secrets just don't remain hidden. Loyalty to voters and the Public in general is paramount in UK politics. You also can do your best to quash any rumours coming your way, in or out of the House." She almost wagged her finger warningly. "New Bills about to be circulated in the House don't suddenly go what yer could call 'silent'! Bear in mind that our dead MP was only sort of 'dispatched' just the night before exposure!"

Chin-wagging but educated women rarely fall silent but the two parliamentarians exchanging confidences did do so; for several seemingly long minutes. Faced by a torrid future in this case of brutal murder, should identified possible offenders be found really guilty by any newly unveiled evidence, both heterosexual work-partners needed time to think over their next move.

"You beginning to miss Pete, Shirl? He Was a well-known womaniser, even to you; So you might not!"

"Yer could say so, Pearl. But there's been so much goin' on that I haven't had the time!" The woman with an almost perfect body figure shook her head in amazement at developments since the murder. "He was such a charmin' man; yer couldn't help lovin' him a lot, even when he showed his affections for others as well!" She, another MP-associate of the murder victim, was single, known to be a close ally of the now dead Sir Peter Clark.

"Then who'd kill him, d'yer think? More to the point, is there someone out there with US on their agenda for bein' got rid of?"

"Yeah, jealousy can be a frightening rage, Pearl! I often thought I could kill him myself for messin' me about with my job in the House here, but!" Shirl shook her head yet again.

Friender looked out of what he hoped would prove to be his *temporary* office. There were flags flying down the street to mark some occasion or other. Then he turned and his gaze fell yet again on all the paperwork. He scratched one ear lobe and chose one of the files wrapped in a large and thick rubber band. He'd now collected basic information on three persons who he'd developed suspicions about in regard to the MP's death. Scanning quickly through the paperwork, he selected a still fairly basic profile on a female currently under police suspicion. She lived in a pretty posh apartment in South Kensington, well known as an affluent suburb in Westminster. Her links with the investigation on the murder victim included quite frequent trips in boats along the river Thames, Westminster Palace parties and very expensive presents. Friender dwelt on an impulse to contact the chief inspector to congratulate him and his team on so much work put in and facts reported, but resisted the waste of his now, to him, highly precious time.

His hand fell next on more recent mail, the latest written account from his own partner in crime investigations, Jeremy Betchner who he had on occasions enlisted for over six years now. Jem came from an agency but Friender used him as an aid because he was remarkably efficient for an 'amateur' private detective. He noted that Jem's file-style report detailed a female MP's movements and activities over the previous week. What significance did she have in respect of her parliamentary colleague's murder? Was she an intimate part of the secrecy currently surrounding the identity of the real killer?

Suddenly Friender's eyes caught sight of the words, 'She often said she'd kill the MP for deserting her up-stream so often.' Jem's words continued, 'Doubt she could've, but you never know in our police-style job!'

That had put the tiger amongst the house cats, so-to-speak! Living doubt was not an entity he liked living with; especially when she, parliamentarian, was still the only suspect he had identified so far. He realised that he had read Jem's report not many hours previously, but had obviously missed such vital words as "boat trips, up-stream, and desertion". His aide had opened up a whole new panorama of investigation that needed to be addressed immediately! But exactly where must he go first to achieve a start that might furnish an answer or two? He selected a personal visit to the site where She lived; uninvited but using an excuse of mutual loss through the murder. But, he mentally chastised himself, there was still the urgent task of discovering exactly what piece of Wildlife Preservation legislature had been on the murdered MP's schedule; that vital clue could well shed some needed light on the exact motive for the parliamentarian being brutally removed from society?

Feeling mentally refreshed, he redirected his attention to swiftly going-through the rest of his mail and messages. One of the pieces of paper might just hold a vital clue that he so desperately needed right now.

The murdered MP had been intimately involved with a new Act to immediately detain and where necessary punish any individual who knowingly harassed or injured a wild animal located inside any one of the UK's parks. This was likely to be hotly debated on more than once occasion in both Houses because of the uncertain definition of "Wild". Many other MPs had seen previews of the proposed wording in the draft and had voiced immensely strong opinions over the need for exact clarification of just exactly which occupants of any officially registered within any park were included. It transpired that Not All creatures in any park would be included in the proposed new Act, and this upset many public, including more than a few of the dead MP's close friends and associates.

The retired special inspector grunted as he pushed all the paperwork before him forward to the edge of his desk. Sizing-up all the plethora of information before him on the desk, just Where was he going to make any headway in solving the identity of a killer?

'Get out; speak to people, check locations,' was the reaction of his experienced Investigator's brain—that's where he had been used to working in the past and where his success lay. Why else had the senior inspector 'called him in' to assist in this murder enquiry?

One hour later, he had traced the MP who seemed closest to the murdered man. He expected little useful information from his ongoing chat with the ageing MP but anything to provide new clues was well worth following up.

"Last time, you kindly volunteered to talk to the police in Parliament, your place of work, you referred to Mr Clark's interests in navigation, steam ships and rivers? Can you give me any more information on these *fads*, so to speak?"

"What you expect? He liked going up and down the Thames by boat, simple. He had a particular affection for the islands, or Aits, and visited several of them quite often when not involved with sessions in the Commons or working on Committees. He was also keen on visiting the canals and waterways much further up the Thames; whenever he had the time.

"But did he have any major outside contacts or businesses out there; anywhere along the Thames?" The investigator persisted.

"Ask his secretary. That's the person who used to work for him."

"I'll have to find her, or him, wherever they've moved to now. I'll have to ask a few questions, when you or I locate them. At this stage no one can be excluded from having done, pardon my crude English, the fatal act!" Friender looked hard into the ageing senior parliamentarian's eyes.

"All in good time!" The MP looked away.

"In the meantime, can you, Sir, think of anything else about the victim that could help or lead us to recommending a police arrest of a further suspect?"

"Peter and I were not as embraced with each other as you seem to make out, Investigator! As I said, find his secretary for answers." The MP walked away through the ornate Lobby, deeper inside the Palace.

'OK!' Friender muttered to himself. "Next stop, the river. One of the owners of one of the river boats might have more detail on Clark's trips up-river. Come to think' he paused his thoughts, 'Who's to say the victim didn't travel *down river*? After all, Parliament kind of lies halfway. The founders of the original Abbey sure had business acumen, as well as strictly pursuing their religion!'

Deeper inside the HoC, unbeknown to the private detective who'd *removed* himself, the MP devoted himself to locating Clark's old secretary to warn him of the investigator's persistent ferreting for inside answers to the murder. The whole House wanted an answer as to *who* but he wanted to distance himself from any more questionings! He had enough on his business list without being dragged unwillingly into murder investigations!

The quay outside very famous Hampton Court Palace was festooned with river boats, waiting for passengers of scheduled trips or new trippers looking for a sight-seeing excursion along the legendary waterway. Friender searched amongst the captains or simple semi-business owners for likely skippers who'd have been familiar with the now dead MP.

"You remember the MP who was murdered a little while ago? Did you carry him up the river at all?" He questioned the captain of a larger river boat moored on the opposite bank.

"D'you know exactly where he used to trip to?" He expected no clear answer, but—

"Up to Hampton, further upstream; next to the Palace that's there, so I heard."

"Ta very much—that's all I needed to know. Good luck with tourists today."

Friender stopped back outside Hampton Court Palace, just next to the small row of shops beside the bridge over the Thames. Looking up the river he could just see Ravens Ait Island, a popular venue for celebratory events. Was this the locale where the dead MP had spent so much of his time? Hampton Court was after all where Cardinal Wolsey, Henry VIII's fiscal colleague was reported to have been murdered, though centuries ago! Too much of an old coincidence, he mused. There were hotels close by and plenty of housing accommodation, if the MP had made friends with locals. He would need to use all his investigative prowess locally to find the answers. Of vital importance, had one of the local residents, especially anyone resident on Ravens Ait, travelled to Westminster to kill the MP? If so, for what perishing reason?

He walked down to the river boats peer to talk to a few of the boat owners lurking there. He simply had to unearth an essential lead to the killer—for Queen and country and Parliament!

"D'you recall the Member of Parliament who was murdered recently. Did he come here much?"

"Remember carrying him in this boat from here to the Island a few times—think he often went to parties there; so rumours insist!" The seasoned face of a boat skipper stared questioningly back at the investigator.

"Just as I've heard too! D'you know if he was pally with any particular natives round here, especially female? I'm looking for a good reason for him to come here so often; all the way from London."

"Nope, can't help ya there. You must be an insurance rep or from the press. I get fed up with you nosey parkers disturbing our peace!"

"Thanks anyway." Friender walked quickly back up to the road leading to the Hampton Court Bridge, crossing over the wide river to get back into his car. His investigative thoughts were questioning if the MP's visits here had any relevance to his demise? He'd be better off back in Westminster to question more persons who'd been friendly or, more important, intimate with the victim. He had minimal time to waste up here outside the ancient Palace even if Kings and Queens of England had ruled here centuries past!

Pearl, long-time lover of the dead MP, sat in the House of Commons looking around the historic (once St Stephen's Chapel) and large, well-seated choir-stalls chamber; deserted for the present; no government admin business right now. This was her major work place but it had taken on a melancholy atmosphere since the murder, out there in a hallway! Pete, she knew, had had plenty of other women but could any of them really have murdered him out of revenge? She must go through the list she had built up, she told herself, otherwise more allegations could fall on Her! That she did not want—she'd moved-on now. But without another mistress to blame, doubt still clung to her life, almost like a silent murder conviction!

She'd start with Maisy Walsh, then look deeper into Leona Black's life and connections with the House. Someone out there knew a lot more than they'd admit! But where to start for a not-so-simple girl like her? Maybe asking some of her acquaintances could give an answer? She'd start with the men she knew well here in the House. Carl had always been close to the dead MP- she'd start with him tonight. Who on earth could have murdered Pete, honest over-worked government servant, as far as she knew?

Friender was, to put it mildly, mighty unpleased to find yet more mail and reports in his temporary office. He'd only been away one day up-river! He abandoned the fresh input into his library of 'sort-it-later', except for one document; a report from his senior inspector temporary boss.

It read: YOU'RE WASTING MY TIME, EX-INSPECTOR. GET SOME PROGRESS ON THE GO, OR QUIT! PARLIAMENT CAN NOT BE KEPT WAITING ANY LONGER; ESPECIALLY FOR YOU!

He had *experienced* rhetoric of very similar vein during his long service in the Force; but he'd left it behind on retirement and hated the prospect of a revival. This case was, as expected when it involved the murder of an MP, mighty difficult to move forward with. 'OK' he addressed his conscience, 'We'd better have Jem Betchner in and find out what he's managed to unearth about the dead MP's last actions in law-making in the HoC.' He bent down to his left to pick up his mobile—there'd been no space to put it on his desk!

"That you, Jem? How's your end of the investigation?" He held his mobile close to one ear.

"Positive, Inspector. I've managed to identify the work on new Legislature for Wild Animals that the MP was working on to present to Parliament. Pretty good goin' I reckon, what?"

"Self-praise isn't a quality I need in you, Jem!"

"OK, OK! But I got what you wanted, didn't I? There is, apparently, almost war in the HoC over differing interpretations of exactly what the dead MP's aim was regarding Wildlife."

"Come in, to my office, and I'll soon tell you the cold facts on tracking down our killer."

Fifty minutes later Friender had found his working colleague a chair and listened to Betchner's latest facts on the investigation.

"The MP was almost ready to present his report on new Legislation for Wild Life when he was murdered."

"But why would his adversaries choose that moment to eliminate him? And how many were there in the HoC, d'you know?"

"How can one know, clever inspector? The HoC is a pretty secret place, especially when it comes to revolutionary new bills being drafted!" Betchner shrugged his shoulders.

"I think you'd better return there, Jem. We need to establish those *for* and those *against* this new bill. Then We can straight away eliminate those 'For' from our investigation—makes life a lot simpler don't you agree!"

"How'd yer know which of the select few actually did the killin'?"

"Leave it to me, Jem, 'cos that's when I go back to the Met and *call in the cops*!"

The retired investigator debated, once on his own, whether or not to immediately report verbally back to his MI5 chief inspector or to stay as the freelance Loan Tech a bit longer? Since he'd not been assigned an exact profile by the Met as yet, he opted for remaining as the hired hand for now. Off to have yet another chat with his old colleagues, searching for new ideas about how best to continue his unofficial assignment. Nobody else had found the actual murderer, so carry on Sherlock of the Day. It'd be Fantastic to solve the mystery all on his own! Fat Chance!

Chapter 2

Friender left his temporary office and headed for Waterloo station to catch the London Metropolitan train to Hampton Court Palace, Surrey; opened centuries after the Abbey was founded at Westminster. There was in his opinion nothing further to be explored in the city at present. Once seated in a carriage he relaxed and spent his time during the rail journey pondering why so many officers, detectives and down to earth police had failed to find, let alone identify the murdered MP's killer.

The simplest explanation had to be that he had committed suicide by somehow severing the large vein in his neck, his jugular, himself. The mental image that personal verdict created in his mind sickened the investigator. It was yet another reason why he must solve the question of who and, as the senior inspector had pointed out, Parliament was not in any mood to be kept waiting for the covert and totally unexpected murderer of one of their colleagues to be found and apprehended!

He found it difficult to keep his mind focussed on the ton of questions that pervaded every thought that his hyperactive brain generated; so purposely went blank for half of the train ride to give himself a needed rest.

As the train found Hampton Court Station and drew to a smooth stop, he exited and began to search for a taxi. It was too far for him to walk to the big Bridge and Hampton Court Rd, off which he could get onto the island. And he was in a psychological hurry. He directed the taxi driver to Platt's Eyot Island, along the Thames from the Royal Palace, Hampton Court. He had learnt that the Ait was almost famous for the number of parties, weddings and other social events that almost swamped it quite often. Why then would an MP visit it so frequently unless he was a party addict, or unless he met a close buddy so-to-speak undercover? He needed urgently to sort out which, because if a close buddy, he or she might just be the killer; for reasons either connected with factors in the Hampton area or with Parliamentary business back in Westminster that the MP had been closely associated with.

What a puzzle, riddle or enigma he had been requisitioned to solve by the Met police! Small wonder they kept 'giving-up'!

The taxi dropped him at the riverside end of the bridge across to the island: He immediately crossed over the river and walked onto the island to scout around and fill-in some vital basic facts. He needed this data to form a rationale for interrogating locals and visitors about any visits they remembered that involved the murdered MP. A fuller picture than he had managed to build so far concerning the man's reportedly frequent visits would enable a better synopsis to be pulled together. He would then have a much better idea of possible exact reasons for murder.

Dozens of river boats were clustered around the island, on its bank. Judging by the number of homes he quickly discovered, a lot of people lived here; plenty of places for parties! Or to possess a hidcout!

But where could the MP's male or female (more likely from his reputation) close associates be discovered? Friender quickly decided he must head back to Westminster, London to utilise the more solid rock of available information which he was familiar with there. From his office he could track down both casual and deep acquaintances of the murder victim based around the Houses of Parliament.

That he liked the assurance of!

He'd revisit this island complex when he had much more info under his belt, to enable him to perform a meaningful search for a killer, if that was where they were or had been based.

Friender got back to his office just up the road from Westminster Palace. He had initially disliked the room intensely, but it now seemed a lot more "like home" since his trip up the Thames to a lowly populated island. He had worked in this 'province' for so many years that it seemed like

'Home'. He could work out of this department style base much more securely and he hoped efficiently than half-way up the long historic but humanly redesigned River!

He called-up his co-opted assistant on his mobile—office telephones seemed so cumbersome, even to him a well-passed midlifer!

"Jem, are you fit?"

"Yup! Where you been?" The co-opted ex-investigator sounded fed-up.

"Get yerself 'ere, Jem. I need an update report."

Thirty minutes later, by which time he had amassed and sorted all the facts of the case exposed so far, his assistant walked in the door.

"Good to see you, Jem. What you got to report on your ferreting round here?"

"I'll take that cup of coffee you've just offered! Let me sit-down for a moment and I'll give you a resume. Have *you* unearthed a likely killer?" Jem pulled over the only vacant office chair and sat down with a noisy outbreath.

"Nope; I'd have sent you back to your retirement hole if I had!" The Investigator puckered his lips in hasty annoyance.

"OK, OK! I've discovered a promising lead amongst the victim's old cohorts. Beat that!"

"Give us more? Come on!"

"One of his MP close-friends: She, don't be surprised, worked closely with him on the new Bill, until his demise. He, apparently claimed total credit for the preparation of the report about to be presented to Parliament—which upset her big enough to make her violently angry!"

"So, you reckon that means she's now Chief Suspect?" The Investigator stared at his colleague with disbelief.

"No—but Selene Teemore is someone to be followed up. I've already got her under close scrutiny."

Friender paused before adding more comments or questions. His brain needed a second or two to analyse better the info that Jem had just informed him of. Was this just a loose lead or was Jem in fact making some much desired progress? Time and events would tell, but for now—

"But just how close as friends were they? As much as that lover of his in parliament called Pearl?" The investigator almost leered at his co-worker. "We've reached that point in any investigation, Jem, where verified facts count for more than bright ideas, conjecture or wise notions."

Jem Betchner lowered his head to gaze at the office floor. "Granted, but at least we've now got some real suspects; not just conjectures, as you put it!"

"That's fine, Jem, but we're dealing with the murder of an MP. Parliament are quite literally shouting for an answer as to who-dun-it? And the HoC is reported to be at war so get back to your best scouting for Real details of your so-called suspects; we can then tackle each one face-to-face."

As he left the office five minutes after Jem had left, a short barrage of earthy potatoes was launched at him from the street outside. They were large enough to hurt if they struck and he ducked quickly.

"Mind your own f**ng business, nose-ache. Keep away from us girls, d'ya hear!" The co-investigator suddenly realised that it was women throwing veg weapons at him, not as he'd expect men!

They must be mates of some of the parliamentary workers he'd been inquiring into—he had to admit, fairly meticulously.

"Sod Off, or I'll fetch the police—the men in Black!" He retreated back inside. The whole investigation into the MP's death had suddenly begun to turn nasty! What if the next barrage of hand-thrown artillery took the form of knives and other metal projectiles? Such behaviour was pretty frequent now!

Safe from violent women inside the shelter of his office, Friender planned the next move in his search for MP Clark's killer. After just being pelted by them on his doorstep, it would clearly be unwise to do any immediate investigation of Westminster women in the MP's life. So which line of investigation should prove best for him to pursue? He was clearly now a labelled target, so needed to tread with absolute caution. Yet, he had been signed up by the Met to solve a murder mystery, so that task was his sort of affliction for the

Now! And if he was to heed the female mistrusts somewhat violent warning, then he'd best follow up on all the male suspects he'd logged into his office desk computer.

Where to? Westminster for the best leads at the moment. He grabbed his leather anorak from the hook on the door and exited swiftly. If he didn't furnish a list of viable suspects to his inspector within 24 hours, the Met would terminate his short-term contract! Any thought that he, ex-police detective, might be responsible for leaving the murderer free on local streets shocked him. He must do better than just tolerate such a Total failure on his own part!

He was about to re-enter the Palace of Westminster, to cross the threshold of the historic Central Lobby, when his impatient brain dramatically framed an ingenious plan. Who might actually be in possession of more facts or acquaintance of the murder victim than everyday workers throughout parliament? Such entities as guards, keepers, guides, secretaries, helpers and so on? He must find and question as many of these as he possibly could in as short a time as possible.

The single greatest problem he faced, he knew from long experience in questioning others, would be stubborn reluctance to discuss a dead man; Especially a murder victim! A stabbed MP was Never going to be a popular topic of impulsive conversation. Best starting point would be the canteen facility; people were always more amenable with food or drink in hand!

"You remember MP Clark, who horribly got murdered here?" Friender enquired of two parliamentary workers seated against the back wall.

"So?" The reply was swift and yielded absolutely Nil information.

"I'm just trying to gather enough info to put together a clue as to why anyone would want to commit such a heinous crime. The murder squad in the Met police seem lost. I'm just intrigued about the whole episode inside here, Westminster." He forced a smile at his audience of two.

"What's it to you?" Friender instantly recognised the tone of 'Get lost!'

"OK, you obviously didn't know the dead MP, or see fit to remain disinterested. Is there anyone else in this canteen that you know was familiar with Mr Clark and might be more willing to chat with me?" He began to rise off the simple style wooden chair.

"You're wasting your time, stranger. The whole affair's long dead as far as we're all concerned!" With that the speaker himself vacated the room.

The ex-inspector was not really surprised. Murder always had a habit of maintaining peoples' silence. Reflecting for a minute as he got up, experience reminded him that the most obvious routes to follow in any investigation often proved in the end to be the least profitable data-wise! He had to admit to making a serious mistake in his approach to unearthing likely killers of Clark MP. He must speedily determine other avenues of enquiry.

Gazing around the truly vast hall he had come back to, Friender felt momentarily part of the history of England; monks, religion by Cardinal Wolsey, royalty in Henry VIII, over centuries. Shaking his head he forced his intellectual senses back to reality today. He decided Westminster had no more *now* value in his quest for that vital clue to a murderer. He had uncovered two female flirts who had been intimate enough with the MP to revenge their rage if Clark's love life had strayed to yet new acquaintances!

He must go back to that island in the Thames, upstream from the City and Westminster, to make deeper enquiries about exactly how the murder victim had spent his time there. Fun and parties may not have been core to his main intentions during the last weeks before his brutal murder! And had he begun to develop more close friendships out there that needed urgent investigation? Friender hoped he was the man to find-out.

As he exited his office, briefcase in hand and mind brimming with new questions, he was unaware of two pairs of prying eyes down the street, closer to Westminster, watching for him. He had through his nosing about inside parliament generated two virtual adversaries. If they had murdered the MP, might they now have their sights set on him?

On the train out of London, Waterloo, Friender sat opposite a man whose attention was wholly concentrated on reading a paperback which bore the title of 'A Murder to End All!'

"That paperback should keep you well occupied for the complete journey to Hampton!" he remarked. "Quite a setting itself for murders in the distant past!"

"You a historian or something; then again, maybe a snoop?" His journey companion puckered his nose in disdain.

"You could be half-right. I'm interested. Know much about the subject, yourself?"

"I've vaguely looked into one or two."

"So, you police?" The investigator asked not too enquiringly.

"Retired." The stranger's response was dry.

"Mighty strange; that's my status too." Friender paused to assess his best response to follow up on the lead offered unexpectedly by his travel companion. "You must be familiar with the recent murder of an MP, then?"

"Yup, but keep your voice low. Public can be an unwanted nuisance."

Friender raised his eyebrows and nodded at the valid warning.

"Your case?" the stranger asked.

"Not when, as mentioned, I'm retired. But I've been called in as a reserve to assist. You got any links to the incident?" He just wished his retired colleague would reply in the affirmative.

"No chance—I've no connections to the Met on that one! You've sure landed yourself a big one! Know the Detective Inspector well, do you?" The stranger looked slightly puzzled.

Friender shook his head. "No, but he knows of me. You remember how hierarchy always 'knew it all'!"

"Yup." There was no expression of surprise or question. "I had a like case some time back: woman stabbed her mate along the canal. Dragged body it into the bush down the bank.

Not like yours taking place in the no less a location than the House of Commons!"

"We all get sent the case that baffles us. Thanks for listening."

The train pulled into a station up the line and his temporary companion exited, wishing Friender Good Luck.

He got out at Hampton Court and headed for the bridge as quickly as his not so young legs would function. The island he wanted to re-examine was only a quarter mile upstream along the Thames. His mind, still adept at investigating for clues, was gripped by the facts only just supplied by his police co-worker met on the train. A female assassin had murdered on the bank of a canal and had then hidden the body. Was this useful data in his current quest for the MP's assassin? His investigative expertise was temporarily stumped by the enigma such a riddle of a question posed.

Chapter 3

Friender stayed in his Westminster Office for most of the day. The whole experience of the journey to Hampton and Platts Eyot in search of a murderer had taken a hefty toll on his ageing energy reserves. Analysing, for the umpteenth time, the information he had gleaned so far, he was beginning to formulate an ever more complete portrait of the murdered MP. Clark had been a model member of Parliament, supporting good causes and a strong package of legislature that governed the country well. But his one weakness or failing was love of the opposite sex. Could this knowledge, the investigator asked himself, yield enough insight into the MP's circle of intimate friends to point a strong enough finger at a likely or probable assassin?

And yet he must not overlook the vital feature of Clark's Bill, which was to protect wildlife in parks. For what reason had the MP thrown his weight and influence behind writing the bill and pushing so hard to get it approved by the House of Commons? He'd antagonised a lot of people in his efforts to gain recognition from the wildlife lobby; including a possible killer?

Unsolved dilemma; which aspect of his work and life as an MP had the assassin been most upset by? Could he, Friender private hired investigator, be perceptive enough to identify the individual who most hated Clark; enough to murder him? MPs were renowned for receiving a continuous barrage of hate or threatening mail from every branch of the population that they served.

Where next? He must put more into sussing-out Clark's colleagues and work-mates; most importantly to dig out any facts the police originally investigating the murder had missed. He had no alternative but to go back to the senior inspector on the case and have a deep chat. The inspector hadn't managed to solve the murder himself but he'd know a lot more about persons involved than most other people.

He managed to track down SI Peterson fairly quickly through use of his old contacts still in the Met. They met at the back of a pub in Westminster, set back a little from the Thames.

"Good of you to come, Inspector. I now being merely a civilian investigator had to consult you as my Force supervisor. You already have my first informing report so perhaps I can ask your advice and run-down on any new evidence the Met has come by? As I summarised in my report, I've managed to narrow major suspects down to two women here in Westminster with whom Clark was very familiar; maybe one or two upstream on the Thames, and possibly an MP or two right here in the Minster."

"You've made fair progress, Tom, I have to say: Even when you've been attacked by women in Westminster parliament!"

"How in the Commissioner's name did you know that?" Friedman was almost shocked.

"You forget, Tom, that murder of an MP is high level crime. We've got a watching eye on you!"

"You expecting me to actually solve the case, or something?!"

"Frankly, from your performance in past investigations, YES! Why else would I take you on board my team so late in the inquiry?" The inspector scrutinised him questioningly.

"I'll take it as a complement. You got anything to give in exchange?" The investigator strongly doubted such providence—policemen, especially ones of rank, rarely gave anything away!

"As it happens, Tom, yes I have. Our further enquiries have indicated that the MP's closest business links were not in the House of Commons but on the Thames Island upstream he lived on for a good part of his recent life."

"Why d'you find that an important aspect of his murder?" Friender was puzzled.

"Because, if it is the case, why go through what must have been a mighty challenging plot to kill him in Westminster?"

The investigator nodded. "And that asks the question, how many people were actually involved? One murderer is hard enough to track down. A team presents far more of a challenge to the police and to me working on my own."

"But you don't have officialdom to cope with—you well remember I'd think." The senior inspector on the case raised both shoulders.

"Yup, sure do!" Friender raised his shoulders too. "Your team got any useful new leads to possible suspects? I didn't have enough time to make much progress with identifying close friends or alliances on Platts Island, or in the Hampton area generally."

"Then get back to that region of enquiry and dig hard for more clues, Tom. We expect more leads from you, being independent, than you've identified so far! We need to lay the murder investigation finally to rest fast as we can. Parliament's still hurrying us every day of the week!" The inspector half held his hand out as if expecting an immediate response from his single audience.

"Working on it, Sir!"

"You'd better be, to keep your contract as the investigator!"

They parted amicably but with urgency, a vital target for the immediate future.

So where next? He asked himself silently. At that moment his mobile phone bleeped.

"Hallo?"

"Get yourself OFF the murder!" a female high-pitched voice screamed into his ear. "If you can't get the message, expect serious trouble until you do! The MP might not be the only idiot killed. Get it?" The menacing near scream ended with a guttural clearing of her throat.

"Can I ask who's calling?" He attempted to calm the caller.

The woman noisily cleared her throat again. "You find out! That's what you're paid for!" The mobile connection died.

Was she the murderer he was looking for? Or was she a self-appointed leader of a murder squad? Either way, how was he to going to identify her and perhaps solve the murder mystery? That's exactly what Inspector Peterson had virtually demanded only thirty minutes ago!

Following-up on an instinct that the caller was part of the House of Commons Gang, as he now named them, he simply had to get back into Parliament. Only, as the inspector had inferred, if he ferreted a lot more into the dead MP's old buddies and acquaintances would he find the new pieces of evidence he so desperately needed to finally expose the likely killer. Since Urgent was now his middle name he simply must get on and interview More potential suspects, even if it meant possible lethal assault inside the House while he was investigating. He had trained in combat in his service with the Met, so he was competent to deal with any attacker; even an irate female! Death threats were an *item* in the daily schedule of a Met detective!

He still marvelled at the incredible gothic architecture of Westminster Palace as he went back to his current work point off the Grand Hall. He first needed to flush out the senior parliamentarians or secretaries who had worked for MP Clark before his murder. Deeper questioning of them might just uncover clearer leads to the assassin he was searching for. Since the MP had been killed inside these very walls, he'd better keep a very sharp eye open for anyone who had plans to dispatch him too!

"Are you familiar with, or more deeply in the know about, the dead MP's writing plan for the Act of Parliament he was working on? Something very closely linked to wild life I heard." Friender had located a parliamentarian who once had been more than just mildly friendly with Clark.

"I should be since I am still a member of the team bringing forward the potential Draft Act. We now have reached the Report stage and hope to progress on swiftly as poss. That will achieve two things in not only recognising the hard preparatory labour put in by the victim himself, but also should hasten achievement of better legislation to protect wild life in Parks."

She nodded, as if expressing a little self-praise for speeding the Draft Bill through its many official stages inside the House of Commons.

"But, forgive me for keeping on, can you recognise any solid explanation as to what reasoning lay behind MP Clark's murder just because he spared no effort in bringing forward his Act; one might rename it?"

"Don't try and drag me into your inquisition! I just worked here with the man. We've got enough legislative action to keep us over-busy without people like you ferreting!"

Various other workers, officials and general parliamentarians in the Palace who the investigator questioned had nothing to add to the data he had acquired so far. To label him as frustrated hid the depth of work and his personal investigative skills that he had employed so far. As his temporary new boss kept emphasising, Parliament would not wait! So if he had to make a red squirrel-style jump to make some further progress, where to next?

People he could still chase offered a thousand new branches of the mystery tree; but which if any would provide a fruit-bearing advance for him to land on? Trying to advance a murder investigation inside Parliament was seemingly impossible for a retired investigator!

As he yet again left the train from Waterloo to Hampton Court to revisit Platts Isle, Friender shook his head and sighed at what seemed an impossible task just ahead today. He loved treading the bank of the Thames and getting onto the Island once more, but scenic visits rarely gave an investigator the vital leads he, or she, needed to complete a case. And that he was under increasing pressure to do or earn heavy criticism from the forces of parliament he was supposed to be helping to resolve the unexpected loss of their work comrade in the House.

Platts Isle stood in the middle of the Thames as splendid as ever; occupied with houses and skirted by river boats. How could there ever be a murderer in residence on such a tranquil location? Such a twisted member of the local peaceable residents must surely be based back in London? But his police instinct, though retired, prompted his conscience that he simply had to finally tie-up this end of the dead MP's life before he could proceed with more prying interferences back in the vicinity of Scotland Yard.

"Oi!" a nearby male voice shouted at him. "What you keep snooping around our charming island for?" An aggressive looking but obviously wealthy man confronted him near the water's edge. Not so weirdly for an island peppered with mini-gardens, the stranger carried a sharp tool.

The investigator took an instinctive step back. "I'm under a lot of pressure to help the police solve the crime of murder of your MP."

"This ain't the dead man's constituency, Snoopy! Go look elsewhere and leave us quiet citizens alone! You're making too much disturbance of our peaceful and safe environment. I'll ring the commissioner if you don't leave us alone!" He stepped back almost too close to the river in token gesture that the matter was closed.

"Sir; you help us end the mystery of MP Clark's murder and I'll be off your island at once."

"You and your mates have pretty much dug up our small piece of land and pestered everyone living here. What more d'yer want?" The resident's manner was now dismissive.

"To uncover a killer! You know if anyone's found an implement, kitchen, garden, anything left lying around that is sharp edged? I'd also appreciate any rumours you've picked up about shady looking persons anywhere near the dead MP's house." Friender shed his coolness and grinned to encourage some response.

"The detectives here some time back now covered all those things!" The resident screwed up his lips in disbelief at the investigator.

"Yes, yes, of course! But I'm one of the also-rans who follow up a case investigation just to make sure some facts haven't been missed. You can trust me!"

"If so, stuff this into your case bag. Dave, who lives about seven properties from me says he saw two stranger girls hanging about a few days before Clark had his neck slit open! Get that nosey ex-cop!"

Friender felt his heart almost leap out towards the informant. If true, such new material was the best data to come his way in weeks!

"Did this Dave give you any description of the two ladies? That would be priceless detail to aid me in finding them. Thanks very much for helping." The investigator kept up his charm.

"Nope! Typical of the MP's usual floozies he said. He did little to improve the quality of life here on the Ait, I can tell you!" The stranger's facial expression conveyed his antagonism.

Having interviewed a dozen or more of Clark's fancy women, both here on Platts and down-river in Westminster, Friender already had a fair picture of what the two probably looked like. It was beginning to look very much like the MP had in some strange fashion worked in pairs for his sex life. Whether two women at once nobody, including the fancies themselves, had mentioned!

"So what we don't know is whether the MP's birds were from here or brought in or they liked to chase him around the country."

"Your challenge, Investigator. That's what you're paid for!" The fat resident poked a finger at Friender.

"Exactly; and that's why I'm perhaps 'going over Old Ground again' as you see it. Since, I'm thinking none of the MP's fancy women apparently had a grievance with him, then I need to stick to the really important women in his life; put another way, I've got to go back to Parliament."

"Do it your way, copster, although you haven't got anywhere so far challenging the unity of the MPs there!" The Island resident spread both hands out in front of himself.

"I'm not in a confronting mode, Sir. My sole aim, at the moment, is to uncover any info that's available—anywhere!"

"Just make sure you don't so to speak 'dig up' the MP when we're only just getting over his murder and subsequent burial."

The investigator shook his head; "Clark was killed in the House of Commons, and there's not enough land here for a burial!"

"So say you!" The resident turned and left him, returning to the peace of his own residence.

Friender hardly noticed the departure, his analytical mind was suddenly in such a whirl with all he had just learnt. Questions, questions and more questions his reasoning mind complained.

In the relative isolation of the train carriage on his way back to London Waterloo, the investigator as methodically as possible thought over the fresh ideas he had been presented on Platts. Why had the resident referred to the murder in such knowledgeable terms? And, why had he mentioned a funeral almost as if he had attended? These twists on the confidential information he had received straight from the mouth of the senior inspector did not make any sense! Who was seeking to confuse who, and for what possible reason?

Heaven sent he didn't have to pen or phone a reply to anything! Leave it to the clerks. But he Must get back into Parliament and sort-out the precise minutiae of facts connected to the murdered MP's death and subsequent dead body disposal. Surely there couldn't be any confusion right in the centre of legislature and control of the population which the Commons stood for?

But also, his astute brain almost shouted at him inside his head, he must determine Exactly who amongst the MP's previous colleagues was hiding behind the impenetrable complexity of Westminster. He almost began to convince himself that being merely a retired investigator he stood no chance of solving MP Clark's murder, but auspiciously his past master police ego tripped in and dissuaded him from giving in to the tough but Not insoluble circumstances. He'd done it before, which after all Was the basic reason for the Senior inspector to have called him in to the case. So 'Get On' he almost shouted back at his uncertain brain.

Chapter 4

Friender had just entered Westminster Palace once again when he noted two policemen guards detach themselves from the sentry post and move swiftly towards him. They grabbed one of his arms each and propelled him from the Grand Hall down a narrow corridor and into a small interrogation room.

"Sit behind that desk. We've some questions to ask you," ordered the guard with two stripes on his uniform.

"I'm not challenging your authority here," the trapped interrogator spoke for the first time. "But can somebody give me a clue as to what the hell this is all about?!" He placed both elbows on the small desk top to insist he was relaxed.

"You're under investigation for continued, unwanted and shady poking around in here and insisting members answer your inquisitive questioning."

"That's my job. I'm a private investigator hired by your force to find who murdered the MP a few weeks back." He leant forward towards the now seated policemen in slight defiance. Tread cautiously, his police training warned.

The older policeman stood up and looked past his detainee. "We've been warned 'bout your prying habits. You're not authorised to poke around in here upsetting parliamentarians and others. Go outside in future and conduct your questioning and prying out there in public!"

"I assure you I'm not, as you put it, poking and prying into important people in the House here. My task is solely to get enough facts to help us all find the murderer! If I do the whole of parliament's goin' to sleep easier." Friender raised up both palms as if wanting help.

"To repeat, you intruder, not in here! If you come back, we'll get your private investigator's licence taken back too."

He knew from experience this was no idle warning. He had to close the book on the actual murder scene and go find what he desperately sought elsewhere. Without challenging the two grim-faced guards further, he stood up and indicated readiness to depart from the Palace at once.

Friender went to sit in one of the well-kept gardens outside Westminster. His head was literally buzzing with new questions. Where precisely had the MP been murdered? How? now entered the equation. When exactly?—he must go back to the post mortem examiner. Why? Was this the key to the whole nasty event or was there as yet hidden reasoning to the death? And how the devil was he going to provide an explanation to the whole apparently insoluble puzzle?

The two police guards had meanwhile reported back to their superintendent inside the House of Commons. She seemed well pleased at the outcome, but still sought final reassurance.

"You absolutely confident that blighter won't come back snooping again?" She almost appeared willing to embrace the guard in her quest for certitude. But he, old school, backed off as his Superintendent got too close.

"Yeah—he won't be back. He couldn't wait to get out of here to the outside. Snoopers often show they're weak if confronted." The senior policeman clenched and raised one fist.

"Parliament keeps on at us to assure their integrity and privacy; I so nearly said secrecy (!)" She almost grinned. "And don't forget, that's our job here." Both guards instantly nodded their heads in total promise to uphold security. All draft Acts and other businesses in general were totally confidential from the general public; including snoopers prying for hot news. Even Friender, ex-Met was not immune from such a label!

In spite of all the obstacles that seemed to block his progress towards finding the murderer, the investigator persisted in his quest. One of the MPs who belonged to the departed Clark's group or clique or ring of buddies Must know what terminal obstacle had blocked presentation of the draft bill to the House of Commons. Who had stood in Clark's way aggressively enough to murder him? And what aspect of current 'about-to-be' legislature was toxic enough to actually warrant murdering the proposer?

Back to the drawing board he told his experience! If he had now been barred from the work place of MPs, then he had to shift to their Constituencies. Much more wearing on the shoes but the only resort left to further his investigations. Priority? Make a list from what he had dug-up to date. Then find their 'home territories' and go there, one by one. Luckily he had no actual schedule, other than urgency! He'd start with that biddy who'd attacked him inside the Commons, off the main hall.

Kendall, right on the edge of the Lake District, next to Lake Windermere but a million miles from the Atlantic, not far from Sedbergh where he'd been to school; nice town. Next door to the window cleaners, he was sat in a small office waiting for Liz Ritchies, MP.

He stood up to shake hands and spoke first. "Thank you kindly for agreeing to meet me, councillor."

"No problem; I'm always available for my constituents." She sat down on the mini sofa.

"Are you at all familiar with our departed MP's Commons work on protecting wildlife?" The investigator wasted no introductory talk prior to launching into questions. "Perhaps you also felt strongly against his proposed legislature?"

The MP's well made-up eyes narrowed slightly. "You searching for Any excuse to accuse me?" She also wasted no words in striking an accusatory approach to their supposed useful discussion; voter to MP.

"If you had no beef against the victim, perhaps you know of someone in the Commons who did?" She might not be the individual he was seeking, but she could still be useful in his quest to expose the killer.

Her eyes narrowed yet further. "I'm not here to be interrogated by an amateur! You have no idea what you're on about!"

He took the simplest route. "Please Mrs Ritchies, I'm not wanting to upset you in any way. Simply put, your colleague in the House of Commons was brutally murdered. This we all are familiar with. But I'm hired to find who committed the crime. I'm only attempting to, so to speak, draw up a schedule of MPs to enlist for help. Those with only a fleeting acquaintance of MP Clark will clearly be of no use to me. You, I believe, know the others who knew the murder victim well." Friender found himself almost pleading for assistance to attract the MP's aid.

"I Do Not wish to become involved in your investigations Mr Friender! Go and do what you're paid to do on your own! Since I did know Peter quite well as a working colleague and we're all concerned with solving the murder, here's a list of other MPs who worked close with him, and me." She had rummaged in her handbag for a note pad and scribbled a list of names while redressing him. This she pushed towards him.

"OK I'll speak to them in the hope someone can provide the information we all need."

He had returned to his office, a long way south from Kendall, after convincing himself he needed time to properly analyse each of the names the MP had given him. He had learnt over his time as investigator that reckless speed in his work got nowhere. Sorting data and finding vital clues were painstaking operations. Above all, very little could be accomplished these days without the use of computers—everywhere people walked about with a mobile phone plus minicomputer or just a minicomputer on its own. The human brain was almost a dead entity!

Of equal if not greater importance was protecting oneself against backlash, especially from those accused persons who would not hesitate to kill again in order to eliminate further threats to their integrity. Friender had no desire to join the murdered MP in a grave! He intended to unearth the murderer without risking his own life.

The major question he must resolve was 'which MP, of those listed on the scrap of paper given to him in Kendall, might have murdered Clark out of rage over some as yet indefinite aspect of the new Bill of Parliament that the dead MP had been working on?'

Who could give him valid answer to such a fundamental query? He was not allowed back into the House again, so go search for more clues around the MPs' constituency offices, around the country! At his retirement age he was no longer a keen traveller, so the prospect held no excitement. But since he was now the sole investigator actively working on the case, he had to go!

Would travel outside the city offer escape from the angry gang of MPs who had threatened his survival? He could only find out by going to Bristol, home of a listed MP, for a day-or-two. As he exited the office, he knew eyes were watching! Such notoriety was not pleasing, made more so by his uncertainty of who, police watchers, MP's protectors or spies he had never thought of. He knew he was a 'marked' man', not a status he had ever risen to before; not even in the London Met!

Sitting in a street café directly facing Clifton Suspension Bridge he waited for the local MP who had agreed to meet him briefly, to clear her name.

"What've I done to make you suspicious of me?" She was a plain but boldly decorated person. Friender was attracted by her brash attitude.

"Nothing! I've a list of MPs who 'knew' MP Clark closely and I'm seeking to eliminate all those who obviously have no connection with his murder: Not easy with Parliamentarians I'm finding!"

"Where d'you want to start with your hostile interrogation? You look a nice enough chap to be so anti-politics. Begin by telling me who's on the list and what you want from Me."

Friender had to keep reminding himself, as an investigator, that he was interviewing MPs more to analyse their personality or character than to cross-question them about events in this preliminary stage of enquiry. Who as a politician would consider wielding a very sharp implement that they were carrying, with the sole intent of actually killing a colleague; simply because they angrily disagreed with the attacked person over the content of a lawful Act about to be passed in Parliament? A conundrum!

He had a long way to go to find his murderer! Amongst the riffraff in the back-streets of Camden Town, not hard to find a would-be killer. But here in the learned Houses of

Parliament, it was going to be near impossible to identify a murderer, if one even existed.

But admission of defeat was not an option as yet—press on Investigator he badgered his persistence nature. Which MP next, or was he orbiting an empty planet as far as available data for naming the murderer?

"I've asked this question dozens of times, but no one's giving a logical answer yet. Exactly what wording in the draft Act that Clark died formatting was so disturbing to the murderer amongst you?" Friender raised his eyebrows.

"I've no idea what you're talking about! None of us plotted to kill our colleague MP. So why should we, as you infer, have any idea who actually murdered him and why?" She leant forward to stand up.

"Please, a minute or two more!" the investigator held up both hands. "If, as I've heard, the murder victim was working mighty hard on protecting true wild life in our National Parks, so who could possibly wish him dead to pay for that status for so-to-speak Stray wild life?"

The MP looked at Friender in pitying fashion. "You seriously, with your awareness of Parliament, still believe like a common citizen that new Acts are simple and straightforward in their preparation and approval by Parliament? Each takes a mountain of effort by the involved party, and this quite naturally means hot competition. Get Wise Mr Interrogator!"

"I think I see where you're coming from, My Lady. And thank you so much for being open with and helpful to me. I'll pass all this information on to my boss, the Chief Inspector."

Chapter 5

Now retired Chief Inspector Friender, currently private investigator, reported back to the special branch inspector who had hired him.

"I've looked at this case from every angle, Sir. Generally, the people I've interviewed or chatted to have been helpful, although more than a few have objected to continued interrogation and what they see as an interference in their lives."

"Nothing new, Tom. You should be familiar with all that having been with the CID for many long years. What I need is a resume of your findings in respect of the murder of the MP?"

"As your reports from CID and others have advised you, the MP was murdered by a cut down each side of his neck so he quickly bled to death. The body was found in the House of Commons, no distance from where the MP worked, when not attending a session inside the Hall. A detailed investigation of the incident by the Met unfortunately provided no clues to who might have committed the murder. I personally, Sir, add to that, 'or Where'."

The inspector pounced verbally on Friender's observation.

"Where? He was murdered in the House of Commons, surely? I advise you not to complicate the murder mystery anymore by adding more unknown and unanswerable queries to the current enigma!"

"Apologies! You certainly have an apt command of English, Sir."

"You're only adding to the mystery even more! Just where are you suggesting investigations should spread to? There's only a very limited manpower left on the case, remember. Since the MP's mutilated body was discovered in the Commons Hall, where the hell to next?" The inspector scowled and grunted his disapproval of Friender's new suggestions.

The private investigator immediately sensed that he could anticipate no assistance from the Met, or probably even less from the CID. But he had a contract to fulfil, so he'd better get on with it!

"Hoping for odd bits of info in return, Inspector, I'm gradually forming the view that more than a few aspects of the case, as built up by the police, are wrong. There's no hard evidence that MP Clark was actually attacked in the House, nor that only a single person was involved. Drawing on those conclusions for the time-being, I've stretched the remit you gave me to cover a lot more people involved and perhaps many sites." Friender halted his admission of stretching his fields of investigation, to stare at the inspector, his boss, for approval.

"You being freelance, Tom, I've got nothing to say. I brought you into the case to use your talents for answering mysteries which have stumped us in the past. So, get on with it! I don't need unsolved murders on my books and I'm looking to you to uncover the vital clues we need to solve this one! MPs don't get murdered every day!" The inspector turned as if dismissing the case.

Since he was no longer allowed to keep going back to the Commons to interview more persons working in Parliament, or to revisit the number one murder scene, Friender went to the New Scotland Yard Crime Museum for inspiration. Notorious cases in the past, including their murder tools, or the vitality of forensic science today might inspire him. Better he reasoned in his head than sitting in his office pondering *ad nauseam*!

Paintings and statuettes of women inside the museum reminded him that the murderer he was hunting for could be either sex. Females were more and more overtaking their male counterparts in organising, controlling and overseeing—even dictating the way forward! Had the true motive behind MP Clark's murder been no more complicated than vying for the womanising MP's full love? Nothing related to politics and

Acts but purely competition between admiring women for Clark, Clark and more Clark!

Yet, again his experienced mind was working full pitch, he must not discard at this middle-of-the-road stage in his murder investigation, possibilities that Parliament itself or rivalry over getting Bills or Acts published or deadly rage over some insult, could not be essential factors.

So, who? Were those two women based in Westminster he had briefly scrutinised early in the case? One was Pearl, the MP's assistant, who had assisted him in his initial investigations. Come to think, she had brought up a Selene Teemore as a long-time lover of the MP. Jem had also unearthed that in his prying around. Good lad! Which one to reinvestigate first? There was a limit to time available, even for a private investigator! Better go for the MP's assistant first. Where was she now that her boss was deep in a grave? Had she been one of a string of lovers or just neutral—he could not remember off the cuff. Go find her, Friender, or earn more of the inspector's disgust at lack of progress!

He found her through a tedious search on Google, though it only actually took a few minutes. Pearl had relocated to MP's office of legislative enquiries. Without hesitation, he rang her and invited her out to lunch in Birdcage Walk, just up the road.

"Did you, or a group with you, kill Sir Peter Clark, MP?" He used as soft a voice and as charming a questioning as possible—the last thing he needed was to antagonise her.

Pearl was instantly on the defensive, but not, he was pleased, on the counter-attack.

"Why would I murder the man I admired and liked working with?" she responded. "Whoever you find in the end—the murderer—they need hanging themselves!"

"I'm not in that job, myself! I know you've been asked a dozen or more times, but have you recently thought of anyone who might have wanted to kill Peter because of some disagreement? An MP must receive threats all the time!" Friender needed to literally bleed the prime witness right in front of him of almost anything she knew of the MP's enemies.

"Have you recently been in contact with Selene Teemore at all?" He had a sixth sense impression that Pearl just might be useful to use as the contact to his next interview.

Friender traced his next prime suspect to a large newspaper's offices in Fleet Street. Once he had established contact, he invited her out to early dinner, before she journeyed home to Hemel Hempstead, northwest of London. The investigator had concluded that the murdered MP's most logical killer was not his chief assistant in the Commons, Pearl. This assumption, he rarely abandoned any witness as a suspect, meant that Selene presented heightened importance as chief suspect. He must handle her equally sensibly—a deeply suspicious known lover of the victim would be useless as a source of vital clues. Also, since the Met had pumped her dry as to vital leads to the murderer, he faced a near impossible task of getting anything new from her.

"Since you girls are renowned as speedy talkers, especially on such a hot topic as murder, I'll start with the same request I put to Pearl, did you have any reason to kill MP Clark? If so, why?" He smiled at the quite attractive secretary—lucky journalist who she collaborated with!

As she also most likely replied, "What the hell for?" Selene scowled at him.

"Jealousy, rage, disgust at being treated as his second-class date?" Friender raised his eyebrows questioningly.

"Not enough to murder him. You're asking bloody stupid questions, Mr! He was very friendly and I admired him. Full Stop!"

The investigator sensed he was really wasting time with this very close friend of the murder victim. She surely hadn't enough vitriol in her blood to be a murderess. But? Move on Tom, he warned himself, you ain't got time enough to keep altering your target suspects! Friender's experience was not allowing him any leeway for random searching through the dead MP's huge list of contacts for a chief murder suspect.

He surmised while seated back at his office desk that 'The Two London Girls' were not as yet in the 'likely suspect' list. But his past experience working in the Met as Chief Inspector insisted, "Just put both aside at the present."

Ah! But not in 'the bin' yet part-time private detective. Without having any firm lead on a suspect murderer, he must not yet start eliminating any suspect names from the list he had assembled inside his head.

The sole remaining locale for immediate re-investigation in his hunt for the murderer was Hampton Isle up the River Thames from Westminster. The hunter was changing the suspects he needed to uncover more details about the location where the MP had spent much of his leisure time. He'd have been far more relaxed there, away from the bustle but tight security of Parliament.

Back in a vicinity he was becoming so familiar with, Hampton Court Palace, the investigator sat near the Bridge spanning the Thames and used his mobile office laptop to search out local places and people to interview about Clark's 'happy times' in the vicinity; local police, citizens advice, leisure clubs, time-out event halls, and free rooms too. He must spread his net to capture any locals who knew the victim intimately enough to provide him, investigator, lists of contacts that the visiting MP had befriended over the preceding years, especially sexy women! Never discard any influence of men, he reminded his searching mind. They might kill to get their hands back on a woman straying away from them——Ego must be saved!

After calmly chatting with—he had changed tactics from ex-police inspector style questioner—several of the MP's buddies, Friender suddenly found the very witness he had searched long and hard for. He was in the presence of a male, middle-aged, well-built chap who could not stop chatting about the river canal system.

"Old Clark, bless his spirit, just felt completely at one with the Thames and the whole canal system in this country. There ain't no canals as such round 'ere but he still felt at one with Thames water and the islands along this stretch. There are also forty-five locks which he was always fascinated by." The keen talker paused for the number to sink into Friender's brain attention-box.

"Hence, him living on one of the islands, I suppose? But why was he murdered just for liking the Thames? Makes no sense!" Friender shrugged his shoulders.

"Who knows! Especially when he was killed in Parliament down there." The chatterer waved one arm downstream. "You talked to many of his friends out here? There was I believing some rumour 'bout the MP aiming to get a Bill through Parliament that'd protect wildlife along the canals as well as parks. Now canals are used most for pleasure, like day-trippers, there's more threat to any animals in the vicinity." The newly found middle-aged professional know-all pressed Friender for endorsement of his views.

"One or two. Lucky old me, I've still got a lengthy list of women who knew him well!"

"I'd say it went a fair bit closer than just knowing. Peter showed nil inhibitions when it came to pretty girls, no matter the age!" The not-so-young witness guffawed loudly.

"Keep it down, Sir! We don't want the whole pub to think I'm here just for laughs. Can you fill me in better on Mr Clark's local interests in the Thames and surrounds?"

"He didn't stay much inside his house on the island or Ait. Forever hiking around, often with company."

"Did that include pretty women? I'd have thought they'd make poor hikers." The investigator looked quizzical. He was not finding it easy to build a neat picture of the MP prior to his murder. How in heck, he thought, did one formulate a valid character for a murderer when the matching image for the victim was even more elusive?

"Thanks a hell of a lot for your assistance, Sir. I must be back to base to dig up more facts associated with the MP and his murder. Keep fit. Tarrah!" The investigator turned towards the foot-bridge back to the river bank.

Chapter 6

Friender so disliked his murder investigation office that he often took his papers and mail up the road to the nearest café, where, sat in a corner, he could sip coffee or tea and monitor the mushrooming paper work and mail. Today was little at variance to any other "office day", no matter how cheerfully he read all the mail, reports, instructions or other articles that he had lately received. Only a single envelope and its contents held his interest, but only for a few minutes because the chair next to his was dramatically occupied by a woman. She was strangely dressed in distracting body-wear and her face and head were covered in brightly decorated veils and scarves. She quite literally had incognito dumped herself next to him.

Rather than take defensive actions that were second nature to him, the investigator put on a welcoming posture and smooth talking. "Hallo! Are you lost, confused or looking for a coffee-mate?"

"Don't act the nice guy, Bum! I'm only here to tell a would-be know-all to stop poking into my private life, and that of others; that's my close friends!" The masking almost veiled her real voice as well as her face.

"I know your voice, Selene."

"So, clever dick, I've given you my warning clear and simple. Get out of our lives or risk retaliation!" She raised one fist at the investigator, verbal aggression masking any kind looks she might have possessed.

"I remind you that Parliamentarians are not supposed to raise a fist, especially the ladies! Since you've taken the time to trace me, answer me this. Why was Clark murdered? What aspect of the legislative work you were both involved with made him a target for such retribution?"

"The Wild-life brigade; they want a much clearer definition of 'wild animal' within a National Park, or along canals."

"What difference does it make to the proposed Act?" Friender was wiser than to directly question the MP seated next to him as to which lobby she supported. He had been commissioned, so to speak, to locate and name a murderer rather than interrogate a senior legislative parliamentarian.

"Don't question me on still secret wording of a draft Act! Why haven't you found my colleague's killer yet?"

"A very fair question, Mam, but my investigation is reliant on all persons I talk to giving me honest answers." Friender stared pointedly at the masked woman by his side.

"Pah! You police are useless!" The pantomime creature swiftly stood up and departed in flamboyant anger.

The investigator shook his head almost in glumness at his own incompetence to-date. Where exactly was that murderer right now? And was he now on their murder list if the just-departed parliamentarian's threatening attitude was to be heeded? He had been attacked by a knife wielding villain before in his days with the Met, but he was now older and far more vulnerable. He must, he warned himself, act clever enough to outwit the killer in order to stay alive and working.

To capitulate, Friender reminded himself, he had identified two possible killer suspects at the Westminster end of his investigation. But he could not single-handed pursue deeper enquiries into exactly how closely they were involved in the MP's murder until he had satisfied himself that acquaintances up the Thames River, especially on the islands, were completely 'clean' and guilt-free. So, he had no option but to return to Hampton Court area yet again and research the locals up there who he had labelled as suspects in the murder. Why on earth couldn't the now dead MP have stuck to the Westminster Area, inside the limits of the City of London? But from long experience, Friender knew that the public never obeyed simple rules of society! That's one reason police enquiries took so long.

This time he took the train to Kingston-upon-Thames to avoid anyone who might be tailing him. The walk to Platts

Eyot island was a bit tedious but it gave him opportunity to reassess all his findings to date in his investigation of the as yet unidentified murderer. He now had two female suspects under his belt, both in the Westminster Abbey area. But why then was he here, up-river on the Thames, looking for more likely solid suspects? Find more, his experience warned, and the task of actually identifying the murderer quadrupled in difficulty!

"You heard or found out anything through chats over a pint that's fresh information on the identity of close friends that the recently murdered MP mixed with whenever he occupied his mini-house on the island?" Friender quizzed the landlord in a local pub, of which there were several.

"Since he was killed in London, why expect any suspects to appear out here? You shouldn't rate Hampton as a suspicious area so quickly!"

"Very true, Sir. But no aspect of such a gruesome death is also buried, so to speak, until the perpetrator is identified and arrested. That's what I'm bent on achieving, with your help of course."

"I know nothing about it; take your unwelcome questioning elsewhere!" The bartender almost shoed the investigator away out of the door; well before he had an opportunity to order a pint.

Friender recognised his uninvited status and decided to get out and to make deeper enquiries back on the island. Somebody living there must possess the sort of information he needed to gain better insight into whether Clark MP had ruthless enemies locally. If the murderer Was on the island, he'd better be on constant alert! Killers were not renowned for missing any opportunity to eliminate suspecting police or members of the public who had come-by vital information. If only he was just such a person at this moment, rather than being still in the dark!

Once back on the island, he knocked at several homes, more huts in several cases, and elicited any help occupants were willing to provide. Most he found receptive to his efforts to identify the MP's murderer, but more than a few scowled at him and shut their doors in disgust at being disturbed. After questioning all willing owners for longer than sixty minutes, he paused, sat down on the river bank and took stock of all the information, and chatter, he had gleaned from the island inhabitants. Only one couple had actually confirmed they saw two strangers on the isle around the day of the reported murder in Parliament. He must go back and talk to them some more. They might just remember vital clues they'd not mentioned previously. He'd no other avenue of inquiry to help identify the killer he sought. Yet again, he experienced a moment of disgust at his lack of progress.

The next event drove away any feeling of self-contempt. The moment he stood up and walked towards the bridge off the island, he was suddenly confronted by a gang of men wielding garden tools at him—spades, long-handled forks, rakes, poles and odd hand-tools.

"Get off this island and stop pestering us" they shouted in unison, all tools being poked threateningly towards him. The metal they waved at him seemed somehow to gleam with the holder's angry cut and deep thrust. The inhabitants meant business in their drive to frighten him off their aqueous homeland. This, he warned himself, was much more dangerous than threats he'd experienced up to now. Any one of the weapons brandished by the small but angry crowd could kill him!

Friender then realised that all participants in the hostile group facing him were wearing face masks or overlarge caps or hats. They clearly intended to scare him away! Up to now they had only been demonstrating their antagonism, but how many minutes before one or more began to hurl their garden tools at him?

He immediately knew he'd anticipated the hostile mood right when a trowel was hurled from the back of the small crowd.

"Alright, alright! I'm only trying to solve a murder, people. D'you want the killer to strike you next?" His hands were both instinctively on his hips in defiance.

He quickly berated himself that he was an investigator not an army hero! So Friender turned back and ran to the Thames' bank. He had never been minded to put up a counter-argument to any real danger to himself. Life might be sweet but it was short and needed careful defence every 24 hours. He now desperately needed to plan his schedule of further enquiries more carefully. The quest to identify the MP's murderer would only lead to his death as well if he messed up any further! 'Think a bloody sight more cleverly than you have up to now' he silently admonished his alarmed intellect, hidden somewhere in his nerve-packed brain.

He returned up the Kingston Road to Hampton Court Palace, which he could not stop admiring as the past seat of Kings and Queens of England. Before he crossed the bridge towards the railway station, he searched behind himself astutely just to make absolute sure no-one was following. He had so far failed to locate the murderer. Yet, there was every chance that he or she had identified him as the investigator under police support who was very actively seeking a murderer - them.

Back in his office near Westminster Abbey, Friender pushed aside the no longer voluminous pile of mail and messages to clear his desk. Seated in front of a blank sheet of large notepaper he set about writing out a new plan of action to find a murderer. He had now identified two possible suspects in both the Westminster and River Thames island locations. 2 + 2 he labelled his successes.

But was there yet another killer, or even others he had failed to identify? If he could only rid his mind of this prospect, he could then set about investigating the 2 + 2 in far more detail; hopefully so as to identify the criminal he so desperately wanted to name and see charged with murder. Of course He still had to find solid and irrefutable evidence that any of them actually was a killer! And, before they managed to attack him, the investigator, with every intention of killing him too. Compared with an MP, he was chicken-feed, so Scotland Yard would waste no time hunting his killer! Survival of the fittest, Tom, he reminded his ego, is an axiom to be heeded scrupulously well in this murder case.

The clean sheet of notepaper on his desk was still very blank. What new strategies of criminal investigation likely to yield progress should he adopt? He had only identified four female suspects to date—Why no males? Most vivid details of the actual murder, as reported by the police surgeon, were indicative of a male killer; so why had he unearthed no leads? "Are you too old for the job?" he questioned himself. "Likely" was the immediate response in his logical thinking. "But I'm not giving in, yet!" his ego responded.

He simply had to mentally revisit his days in the Met. Since retirement, the far easier work he'd taken up as a private detective, to keep himself occupied, was of no use in a full murder enquiry! Go back to the detective superintendent in charge of the Homicide investigation, Friender. He would consult the Commissioner as necessary and between them and their teams they should resolve the puzzle of which aspect of the MP's murder he, retired detective, should investigate for missing clues to ultimately expose the vital evidence leading to the killer that everyone urgently sought.

This was all proving to be the biggest headache he'd ever had workwise. How in hell was the person who murdered no less a public figure than a MP keeping hidden from public exposure? Were they extremely clever or were all those hunting them just plain missing the vital clue as to identity?

Scotland Yard headquarters on the Thames Victoria Embankment was nothing new to Friender after the years he had spent in the Met. But the revolving triangular sign outside, the six stories and the large covered entrance still amazed him. Under police escort from the entrance desk, he was fairly quickly seated in the detective superintendent's office room.

"The Commissioner advised me that you had shown previous expertise in resolving murder inquiries, Tom? We had no success in our look into the case, and hoped you'd help. How come no success, in the light of your previous record?"

"Thank you Superintendent, but I've not to date had any more luck than your expert teams. That's why I'm here, 'cos I have an inkling that blending our two resources might pay off at this point."

"Bit of an unexpected deduction on your part at this late stage, investigator!" The DS's demeanour was brisk enough to be interpreted as hypercritical, considering he'd had a police force of trained operatives available to find the wanted criminal, with no success.

"Understandable, Sir, but give me the opportunity to amend the sorry situation by giving me access to two of your best investigators to perform some research inquiries that haven't been undertaken to the present. As you well know, I have minimal authority in the community, which means the public can challenge or even fight me if my questioning upsets them. And that it has done, mostly because they believe the police investigation of MP Clark's murder is complete; they object to my so to speak re-opening the case!"

"That I can't do!" The DS's reply to such an outlandish request was brusque. "Not until I've consulted the DCI in charge of the murder investigation. I have a strong notion that they'll refer your idea upstairs to the Commander. That could take a while since, as you observed a minute ago, the murder we're talking about occurred a while back."

Friender was too old a hand at negotiation to be dissuaded. "May I remind you, Sir, that you have warned me of Parliament's anger at the delay. I am also warning; I cannot progress identifying the murderer without vital assistance from the police."

"Very well: report back to me in one week. I will by then have allocated two officers to assist you, but they will remain under My command at all times." The DS was now dismissive. Anybody in authority deeply dislikes being told what to do by minors or outsiders.

"Tomorrow, Sir; Parliament won't wait any longer." The private investigator quickly exited Scotland Yard.

Friender liked to talk—part of his job, to his way of thinking. He phoned Jem, old-time assistant. "My Office Old-mate; I'll work out a suitable pub we can walk to.

"You're setting a tough demand of the DS, Tom. What gives you any grounds for demanding that he gives you staff support?" Jem's head shook as he mentally analysed Friender's recounting of what had transpired during his extra session with his temporary supervisor.

"Since mobs have halted my investigations at both ends, Westminster and the Thames Isle, I Must resort to calling in police assistance. Their MI5 section and others have failed to identify the MP's murderer. So, what alternative avenue can Scotland Yard explore other than that of assisting me? At least I've made some progress towards finding the murderer!"

"You come up with any ideas where or who I should investigate next?" Friender expected little from his assistant but the mere exercise of discussing his current plight would he felt unearth one or more ideas; and ideas often blossomed into new plans for tackling a murder mystery. He knew from long experience, 'when stumped by the criminal', review the whole case again and again—the answer's hidden there somewhere!

"Your old maxim, Tom, go back to square one!" Jem's eyelids screwed up a little as he looked to his partner for a response.

"You might be right. There's more than two or three possibles who I spoke to very early on, mostly linked one way or another with Parliament. You willing to revisit them with me? That way you can monitor me for slip-ups or any bungling mistakes in my actions!"

"Sure."

"I'll see you at the murder site tomorrow morning. Watch you're not followed—We don't want you on the mortuary slab! I personally have become Super-vigilant of all behind me."

What the investigator did not reveal to Jem was that he was now convinced that he was being followed. He had, up to now, not had the freedom to find out who, but he was absolutely Not risking fatal assault—Watch your back retired Chief Inspector—enemies you've created in past investigations could strike anytime!

Chapter 7

Friender shrewdly re-examined the murder site inside the Palace, House of Commons annex, still searching for any meaningful clues. Ace investigators never gave up, and that trait sometimes paid much needed rewards. The same old questions bombarded his cerebrum. Why here? Exactly how had it been effected? Who might have witnessed it but was not stepping forward to assist the police? Was the murderer related to the MP they had so brutally executed? When might he or she strike again? Why, Why, Why?—there was always an explanation—it just needed exposing! It was his job to do so!

"Have yer solved it this time, Mister? You're supposed to be Super-brain after all!" Jem stood beside the private investigator.

"There are facts missing, super-sleuth! There invariably are, and the mystery murder ain't gonna be solved until those vital aspects of the crime are found and interpreted right."

The investigator regarded his co-worker fully in the eye.

"Don't look at me so accusingly! It's your case not mine! If I'm here to assist, let's go through what you might have put-together here."

Friender nodded his head, retrieved a notebook from his jacket pocket and talked through each of his entries with Jem.

"To sum up; Sir Peter Clark, MP was murdered and his body left here in this annex of the HoC. I have identified two possible female suspects here in Westminster, both involved with Parliament. I have also identified two even more unknown female suspects on a River Thames Ait or island. I'm calling it the 2 plus 2 Murder at the moment. It still remains a mystery exactly why Clark was murdered, but the most likely clue involves the Preparation of a Legislative Bill by Parliament. Strangely there appear to be no Male suspects.

I have met increasing objection from local members of the public to my investigations, forcing me to go back to the Police for assistance."

"How's that?" Friender spread his upturned hands towards his assistant.

"Good, But clearly Incomplete!" Jeremy Betchner responded.

"Then we have to string everything together in a clearer framework to lay-bare the unsolved questions. Find the questions at the hub of our enquiry and we've a better chance of resolving them and exposing our answers to the murder."

"As always Sherlock, you resolve our problems so simply! But, you omitted to Add the actual life-threatening attacks you've encountered?"

"Ah! The answer to that predicament revolves around, how much did I upset the locals by subjecting them to my brand of interrogation?"

Jem shrugged. "There's no simple solution to that of course; we're unable to directly read the minds of fellow citizens, yet!"

"You're too lenient! Back to square one, we've still no clues to the murderer. If the Superintendent co-operates and gives me use of two men, I'll ask them to question my 2+2 deeper than I achieved. You and I can then pursue any inspirations we have on our journey to finding the main suspect."

"Wishful thinking I'd say!" Jem shook his head.

"Not, can I remind you, when your life is threatened; not only by a murderer, as well! Mobs are scary believe me!"

"You and me, Cynic, should investigate why he was killed. That should give us some new clues to act as leads as to who." Friender set off down the hallway towards MP Clark's re-occupied office. Hopefully the MP charged with completing Clark's Bill would be out. They could re-question his secretary along the new lines of why, not who.

They found the new secretary replenishing her lipstick in front of a hand mirror. From experience Friender knew this signified nothing other than she had settled in but was bored and dreaming of her boyfriend coming through the door, rather than two old men on business!

"Sorry to arrive in your work place unexpected, Miss. Could you help us with a few facts about the previous MP who used this office?"

"You mean the dead un?" The young woman looked suitably bored already.

"Not exactly; we're hoping for some information on the Act of Parliament he was taking through the House. Are we correct in assuming that you're currently working on the same Act?" The investigator smiled as pleasantly as he could to encourage a useful response.

"He would have had several, major and minor: Which one?" her face did not beam happy collaboration in response.

"I understand it was associated with Wild Life?"

"That Bill has been halted since no MP has taken on responsibility for its further progress through Parliament. No further action will be taken until Sir Peter's killer is named and put on trial for murder. I cannot help you further." Her tone was dismissive—she had had enough of the two meddlers.

Friender was amazed that they had managed to penetrate the inner sanctum of the HoC so deep. He made no fuss about the secretary's cold response and the nuisance duo left her patch.

"Not much achievement so far, Gunga Din! So where is the maestro going next?" Jem's voice was not collaborative in tone.

"Not far, Cynic. Even if you won't back me, I'm moving-on right here. Clark had a particular MP buddy, who I intend to find next. They are likely to know the details of Clark's embryo Legislative Bill and hence the reason why a particular sector in the Wild Life community were so antagonistic against it; may be strongly enough to kill!"

While he searched the very ancient Westminster Abbey for Clark's close friend, who unsurprisingly proved to be a woman, the investigator's mind could not stop delving back into his own past. How in heck was he, long past servant of the Crown in the Met Police, sort of ferreting about inside the building with the highest status in the UK? Crime squad officers were not supposed to openly investigate Members of Parliament in their own offices, inside the HoC! Had he gone clean over the top in poking his nose around the very establishment where the actual Laws of the Land were made and approved?

Not being a policeman, Jem didn't seem to be bothered by the ease with which he had penetrated Parliament itself. "Are we goin' to find this important biddy of yours in, or has she done a bunk havin' heard yer lookin' for er? This buildin's spooky enough without yer leadin' me into every crevice and cleft inside the Abbey!"

They located the Lady MP two corridors away, down on the right. A single knock on her door granted them immediate access.

"Thank you so much for seeing us, Ma'am. Not to loiter and use-up your time, can you advise exactly what the basic concepts of MP Clark's last Bill were? I think they might have been linked to Wild Life?"

"Since it hasn't completed its passage through the House, that information is Not yet generally available to the public. But, since you seem determined to catch Peter's murderer, which I vigorously support, I'll try to help. Haven't you been threatened if you don't give up meddling into MPs' business?" Clark's close associate stared right into his eyes. He'd never felt comfortable with direct female confrontation.

"Yes, that never deters investigators, especially ex-police! Go on, spill it."

"Yes to Wild Life—Peter had set his heart on stopping harassment of any really wild animals inside Parks, particularly where Zoo or normally protected animals were resident. He struck problems or antagonism whenever an exact definition of "Wild" was called for. A Park is regarded as a defined area of land, and many public regard animals living within it as protected, not wild."

"Hmm! I can already recognise the existence of two camps; one for total protection of all animal occupants; the other for only legislatively identified or recognised endangered animals. Many persons strongly affiliated with animals might just have regarded MP Clark as Enemy Number One!" Friedman was only voicing his analysis, not any opinion pro or anti the public's views. He was still left with the unresolved enigma of which camp the brutal murderer belonged to? Also, did it matter?

"I was a working friend of Peter, not his bodyguard! I don't know of anyone here who was mad enough to actually murder him." She had assumed a bland look on her face.

The investigator looked puzzled. Was this MP a just a companion of the dead man or was she one of his playmates, for which he had an infamous reputation? Friedman chose the Direct route to finding the answer. "Were you one of MP Clark's well-known girlfriends?" he asked.

"I'm beginning to see why you, Mr Investigator, have evoked such an antagonistic response to your questioning amongst the public. Your line-of-work may require direct questioning, but your personal approach to finding out truths is very unfriendly, to say the least!"

"I must obviously apologise for being so anxious to unearth and report the murdered MP's killer. But, what Parliament wants, Parliament gets wouldn't you say, Ma'am! You work here; you should know!"

"My work is My affair! Any further questions or can I get on?" The parliamentarian could not be more dismissive. Friedman concluded that she was too hard in demeanour to be a likely mistress, no matter how womanising Clark had been.

"Thank you for your valuable response to my questions. Jem and me will take our leave." The two investigators departed her office, heading back towards the central Lobby.

"We have at last discovered the likely motive! But that does not identify the murderer until we question the ad hoc leaders of each camp, as I've labelled the groups, as to which followers felt most strongly about likely effects of the Bill on wildlife in parks."

Jem responded. "We'd best go talk to a few Wildlife Parks, Trusts, Zoological and Royal Societies."

Friedman had one of his puckered faces on. "We simply haven't the time, Jem. The murderer could have struck again for many reasons by the time we get to just the Royal Society,

London Zoo or Wildlife Trust." The Investigator put out his upturned hands. "Come up with something a darn sight speedier will you?"

"You're the Inspector's selected expert in solving crime riddles!" Jem shrugged.

"Very well, I reckon that sort of enquiry belongs to the two CID detectives I've requested from the Met. They're more likely to uncover background data from routine enquiries than us. Meantime, US goes back to the Data Bank we've collected to explore for hidden leads we've not so much 'missed' as failed to create."

"You've lost your basic police training abilities! You can't start Inventing clues, mate!" Betchner's voice rose and he looked contemptuously at the Investigator, ex-Police.

"Come on, Jem, you know me better than that! I Mean that we go back to the details of the murder act itself, the exact location it took place, precise description of the supposed finder, and all those basic aspects of the case."

"Now you're talking sense!" his co-worker almost seemed to breathe a sigh of relief.

"Come on, back to my office."

"Step one: what details do we have, from the surgeon, of the fatal wound? More importantly, are we dealing with one wound only? It seems so, therefore we concentrate on it."

"What qualifications do you have to interpret the surgeon's descriptions?" Betchner's voice was distinctly accusatory.

"None. Don't play the awkward child at this stage of my investigation! The wound was located on the right neck, half-way between jaw and collar bones. It lay right over the jugular vein to cause maximum loss of blood as quickly as possible. I understand there was a nick on the left neck too." Friender felt revulsion.

"Hell; it must have spurted out like a crimson fountain! Any thought of the spectre makes me sick, sick, sick!" Jem grimaced quite violently.

"You've a right to express your horror. Death must have been swift. That co-worker suggests meaningfully that the murderer possessed anatomical knowledge and some surgical skills. The police surgeon also reports that the sharp instrument was used vertically up the line of the vein so as to sever it in a fashion that caused the quickest loss of blood out of the neck region."

"I've no medical knowledge but wouldn't loss of so much blood so fast mean the MP very quickly wouldn't be able to stand? It might also allow his body to be moved smartly post mortem?" Jem was still grimacing.

"I'm not a medic either, but I expect so Yes. So, to recap, we've got an MP walking in one of the annexes of the HoC when he's suddenly attacked from the right side by an unknown person with intent to kill. The assailant strikes with a mighty sharp weapon which they stab into the right neck and pull down sharply to sever the jugular vein." Friender shrugged as if dealing with fact only and not any sympathy.

"Couldn't he have been just plain assaulted first and the precision severing of the neck done once he was knocked down? That'd make the cutting easier." Jem stood silent, waiting for the investigator's conclusion.

"There's no detail in the report of any injuries on the body other than the blood-letting." Friender's eyes narrowed, almost in expectation of further insights from his co-worker.

"That makes the assailant either filled with hatred Or having the prior skill to perform a cutting operation on the victim's neck. What's your judgement boss?" The co-worker deliberately stared into space, keen not to bias the investigator's conclusion. Friedman's deduction must be wholly unbiased if he was to stick to his new strategy of uncovering the murderer. Jem could if he thought hard just see where the investigator was going, but that wouldn't bring back the murdered MP!

"Either! We've still got my 2+2, clearly separated by several miles up the Thames. But we've not an inkling of what talents or skills any of them have. That's yet another task for any policeman assistance I get from the Inspector." Friedman also looked skyward. Any immediate outcome of the investigation was about as unpredictable as Mars and Jupiter colliding, let alone men understanding the cosmos, co-ordinated as it might be according to astronomers!

"I think, Jem, we'll leave the second suspect here in Westminster for the moment, and journey again up the Thames to Platt's Eyot Island to probe deeper into the two suspects up there; not that we know who they are yet! I've never undertaken such a complex investigation before; Here and There; Him and Her; Then and Now, Where and Why!" Friender sensed he was about to explode with the prime need for answers, answers, answers.

"Don't omit to go see your Inspector and find out whether you've been approved two police detectives to assist." Jem felt tempted to wave his finger at the prized investigator.

Not far away from the two ex-detectives, deeper in the phenomenally vast and historic structure of the House of Commons, Shirl and Pearl were yet again in deep discussion about the future.

"I'm still real scared about them finding out," voiced one of the parliament HoC workers.

"What did we do wrong, Pearl? We only cleaned up round the body to keep the place looking tidy and moved it into shelter! What's wrong with thinking tidy? Anyway, they took him away pretty quick!"

"Yeah, I suppose it was a while ago and we should Stop worrying."

"That's right, Shirl. Mind, I still can't think why anybody would knock-off a real MP!"

"Politics can be real nasty too! I tell you, we need to be on our guard all the time now! They knocked him off almost in broad daylight. Who's to tell they're not waiting for us round the next corner! I don't trust this Palace anymore—it's got too much history of people being snuffed out, some Royal too, to be reckoned as AOK for us simple workers."

"Never mind all that! Where we goin to tidy-up next?" Watch out for bodies!" The two women went on their way laughing down a long corridor of offices. They knew the occupant of each by sight but who they represented and who or what they were plotting to 'get-rid-of' remained highly unknown.

The islands on the River Thames are reminders of when the river was historically no more than a merchants' canal stretching from Gloucestershire to the Estuary on the coast. Platts Eyot or island happens to be large and heavily populated, a result of boat building for coal transport, and even for the Navy before and during the war. On this his latest visit, Friender was determined to explore more the island *itself* rather than the mixed population living on it. Last time, he'd been seriously threatened with weapons by a crowd of locals! Since it remained uncertain whether the Upstream 2 Murder suspects actually lived on the Ait, he had to get the background facts first. That, he assured himself, was what investigators were good at—the interviewing of murder suspects was best left to police! Also, the further away he remained from contact with brutal murderers, the happier he felt.

He took the train to Hampton Court as usual and walked some distance to the foot bridge connecting the island he sought to the North bank of the wide river, built by the Corps of Royal Engineers in the war. He had on a cap and a long floppy raincoat, sufficient disguise he hoped not to alert the antagonistic locals that he was back ferreting around for vital answers. This time, fortunately, not resident-connected answers but those closer related to the island itself. Could he unearth a vital clue to the murderer by changing his targets of search to the Environment in which the murdered MP had spent so much of his spare time? There had to be a simple reason, he argued inside his head, for Clark to come here other than women? There were after all plenty of them around Westminster!

As he crossed the small man-made suspension bridge onto one of the Thames' larger islands, he recalled two things; Platt had farmed it very successfully, hence the naming, and He Must keep a watchful eye open for hostile islanders willing to threaten him again with lethal weapons! He was an investigator, not a Roman centurion come to invade the river—Let me be his ego almost shouted inside his brain!

Chapter 8

Back in his office in Westminster, not long after the excursion up-river, Friender scribbled some notes, more of a list really, covering all the data he had unearthed on Platt's island. MP Clark had obviously used his out-of-London abode on the large river island to escape from his competitors in Westminster and to run his private advisory business. He Must open the first report from the two police detectives that the senior inspector had recently approved to assist him obtain further basic information from unwilling members of the public who knew the dead MP. Unlikely, he mused for a moment, that young detectives would have uncovered any vital facts that he, experienced investigator, had not uncovered earlier, but he lived in hope!

As he read through the first short report he felt amazed by the efficiency of the police detective. He had not wasted any time researching the core of information that the Investigator had already uncovered. Alan Swift reported that he agreed about the House of Commons being a mysterious conglomerate of fact and fiction but tight survival practices. The detective had found it mighty hard to get parliamentarians to 'talk', but almost to the contrary they went out of their way to help in the search for MP Clark's murderer.

Being an 'officer of the law', Detective Swift reported no difficulty in seeking interviews with MPs and HoC workers; but his report did point to an inability to persuade members of parliament to open-up and reveal any secret information they had accrued about their fellow murdered MP or any antagonists that he had met in the House.

Friender did suffer a moment of disappointment that Swift had uncovered nothing new, but give him time he reasoned to himself. The second freshly written account by a Detective Fred Timmon was of greater interest to the Investigator because he himself had visited many of the locations upstream on the Thames. But Fred had not solved the deathly enigma either; so back to his own basic conclusions to date!

The Investigator rested both elbows on his small desk, cupped hands covering his mouth. This simple position helped his thoughts to coalesce about what action to take next. Too early to call the boys in blue yet for a first progress chat. They needed additional experience of the case to frame any useful ideas on the most fruitful route to follow right now.

What leads should he himself follow, garnered from either Westminster's mysterious challenge or Platt's watery mystery? The House of Commons was right on his doorstep, so wasn't that the easiest riddle to investigate and, never too late to regard as vital, the very location where the MP had worked? So Back to that incredibly ancient memorial to Kings and then legislators.

Could he, nosey-parker according to many, uncover a MP murderer inside the rebuilt abbey with all its hallways, corridors, rooms and access routes? Such a feat would not prove he was any good at writing Bills of Parliament, but reveal himself a master of catching criminals.

The few guards on duty in the entrance lobby paid him no attention—there had been orders from Higher Authority to give him freedom of investigation. So locating the murdered MP's close companion was no longer too onerous.

He found Selene Teemore, Clark's old associate in the HoC canteen, chatting with some of her work mates.

"My apologies for snooping into your relationship with Sir Peter, yet again Miss but I need some more information in order to proceed in my quest for his murderer.

"Nosey-parkers don't usually give up or disappear; so I kind of expected you to show again."

"Kind of you to be so understanding, Selene. Can we go upstairs for a private chat?"

Elsewhere in the privacy of a corridor off the entrance hallway, Friender tackled his dilemma of lack of headway in the murder investigation. "In case you're now feeling safer, can I repeat my question, 'Did you murder the MP?'"

"NO!" she shouted. "I did not." Her voice calmed. "Why are you police so inefficient you can't find the murderer? Especially when it all took place right here!" She glowered at him just as defiantly as she had previously.

"Apologies, but I'm the only one still working on the case—Oh! Has a police detective named Swift spoken to you?"

"Yes! So?" The glower came back on her usually pretty face.

"Anything you remembered that you'd forgotten to tell me or the police first time round?"

"No! Why should there be?" This time Selene's face assumed a confused look. That helped Friender greatly in his effort to both understand the dilemma himself and to help the dead MP's associate understand too.

"You asking, 'Why', nails it in one, Selene! The whole mystery of this case of murder revolves around the enigma of a valid reason for Clark's murder, why here in the lobby, how many were involved, and what purpose did his death serve? There are way too many unanswered questions for the appalling deed to be a simple case of death by stabbing."

"What are you on about? My co-worker was murdered right here for something we still don't understand—though I suspect it had a bit to do with the not yet approved new legislation or act." The parliamentarian looked highly quizzically at the investigator, thinking 'What right has he to invade my work space?'

"It's taken me up to now to work out one fundamental flaw in our grasp of the event. It's inconsistent!"

"Explain, Clever Clogs?" Selene was quick off the draw.

"Where's the blood?"

"What blood?—they cleaned up here after taking the MP's corpse away to the mortuary!"

"Precisely—there was no blood around the body. That can only mean one thing—he was murdered in another location." Friender raised his eyebrows nearly through the elevated ceiling to emphasise his appraisal of past events.

"Oh my G--! That puts an entirely new slant on Sir Peter's death. Where – then?" Selene was clearly agitated.

"That's a pretty simplistic summary of the event, Selene. You must Also ask 'Why, How, When, by Who?'. This is proving to be a far more multiplex murder than the police obviously concluded after their investigations a few weeks ago."

"Sir Peter never was a simple man to deal with!" She looked at her interrogator for advice.

"Unfortunately, neither is his killer. But, on the positive side Selene, I conclude that we can eliminate you from the Chief Suspects list." He smiled thoughtfully at her. "That of course means I must move on to interviewing again the other suspects here in Westminster. As well as you, I spoke at length to Pearl, Carl, Maisy and Leona Black. You must know them all?"

"Not as murderers, Mr Investigator. I'm sure I don't need to remind you, the murderer's still at large—and their first target for killing again to protect their identity is you!"

"I'd not forgotten, Selene. You could make a good detective! The prospect of having my jugular cut from top to bottom makes me feel in need of a sit-down! Back to the office. See you." The investigator did feel slight nausea in spite of his hard-earned experience in the Met.

On his way back out the House and up the main street towards his office, Friender got out his mobile phone and rang Alan Swift, police detective allocated to helping him in Westminster.

"Hi Alan, I think it might be a good time to look critically at our joint data we've put together in the Westminster area. Can we meet in Scotland Yard, off the Victoria Embankment?"

"Sure. I'll book an interview room." The PD's response was swift.

Friender suffered many reminiscences on his walk down Whitehall towards his old Met police offices HQ building. Scotland Yard had, he recalled, a colourful history since its inception by Robert Peel under the 1829 Act. But the past was irrelevant today in his quest for the foul murderer of an MP, who had toiled for Queen and Westminster just up the road. He hoped the policeman would be on time for their first review of facts so far uncovered. Particularly since Selene had strongly reminded him that the fiend could well be right on his tail with a butcher's knife destined for his neck!

Alan Swift was waiting in reception, to show him to the interview room he'd booked.

"Any new data you've collected, Alan?"

"I've spent a lot of time on all the prime suspects you named. I think you've been back to one or two?"

Friender was at once urged not to omit that he was back to old times of working with young policemen. But this detective seemed keen and easy to work with.

"Yes, I've just been chatting to an MP, Selene. Don't know what you thought of her but I've decided she's not murderer suspect any longer. That's not to say, as she herself pointed out, she wouldn't kill me for being too nosey in her domain."

"That's a risk of the job! D'you want to discuss my findings, since we're here in HQ?"

"Good of you to prompt me why we're here—I do now have a mind that wanders, like half the population! Let's have it?" The Investigator knew he must bow to Swift's younger and keener observances.

"I've been through the list you gave me fast as possible, and interviewed anyone I judged suspicious. Glad to say I've not met the resistance to questioning that you reported."

"But have you found a likely murderer?" Friender had a now major sense of urgency to resolve the enigma he'd been set.

"Our basic dilemma seems to be that MP Clark, like most MPs, knew Tom, Dick and Harry, to use a worn cliché. Worse still, neither of us PDs has identified a laudable reason for murder! I don't think you have either!"

The Investigator pursed his lips in concentrated reflection on the junior detective's precise summary of the situation. "Agreed. Yet, there is a concise reason why some angry person wielded a mighty sharp instrument to end Clark's life. We need to revisit what exactly the MP was pushing through Parliament for new Legislation and who this would affect most. What kind of relationship he was manipulating with close associates is likely vital also?"

"I'm not experienced in Parliamentary affairs, Mr Friender; can I suggest you research that aspect of the case, while I'll do my very best to expose the MP's relationships at the end, so to speak." Detective Swift looked persuasively at the visitor.

"Done!" responded Friender. "You've had great success talking to potential suspects. So let's call it an agreed way forward for the pair of us."

"I'd better be getting on then." The young police detective rose to return to his workplace, somewhere else in the labyrinths of New Scotland Yard.

"I'd strongly remind you, Alan, that I'm under threat from person or persons closely linked the murder. Now that you're poking your nose around here in Westminster, that threat must extend to you also." The much older and now Ex-policeman looked shrewdly at his junior.

"Thanks for the caution, Sir. I'll keep a close eye on all around me, especially on anyone with a knife in hand!" Grinning, he moved out of the small interview room.

In his temporary office, Friender mentally surveyed his progress in locating and trapping the murderer he had been engaged by the inspector to identify. He reflected that he'd had much quicker success in the past whenever he'd been brought-in by the police to assist in identifying and finding criminals who had cleverly escaped meticulous police identification. He reminded himself that he'd not been clever, just fastidious enough to identify the really vital facts behind case histories. With these fine points in hand he'd found solutions in each case that had long thwarted the police detectives.

His mind was now swamped with questions, of his own making. His chats with Parliamentary workers had revealed that MP Clark had been hard at work on a draft Bill intended to outlaw any attacks on wildlife that might be discovered in National Parks. The proposed draft had been controversial, according to the format that influential members of the community approved for the term "Wildlife". This controversy was still regarded as the root basis for murder of the MP. The Investigator reminded himself that his experience did not allow such simple deductions. Some factor based on cause and effect of the murder, but hidden from easy exposure, did not allow such an easy conclusion.

Mercifully, the how had not needed any resolving right from the start of the police investigation. But the four 'W's' remained mysteries—Who, Why, Where, and When? These unsolved enigmas were the cause for his summoning by the MI5 senior inspector. Was the murderer so obsessed about the MP's drive to get a new law enacted that they were driven to kill OR had they killed for more personal reasons? The Parliamentarians he'd questioned had been singularly unwilling to discuss such 'un-public' data.

So, back to you amateur Sherlock! But 'One-step-at-a-time' Friender cautioned himself. That's paid off in previous cases. Where to next? Ah! I haven't yet had a briefing with the other policeman, Detective Fred Timmon, up-river. Hopefully he might have garnered background data from pleasure loving islanders up at Platt's Ait as to exactly why MP Clark had possessed such a fascination for women? He reminded himself that Tagg's Isle closer to the Palace down the Thames was a location he must visit and research as well. Clark had been reported to visit there not infrequently; with or without his women!

Chapter 9

Police detective Fred Timmon had felt some elation at being seconded to a special task force; to assist in more detailed probing into facts surrounding death of an MP, no less! It had not taken him long on the job to discover that the MP had in fact been murdered inside the House of Commons: what an extraordinary situation!

Like everyone else involved in the hunt for a murderer, he kept asking, "Why?" But that was his new task, to dig out the facts veiled in the Platt's Eyot area that might answer the enigma. And to add to his challenge, another detective was performing exactly the same task down river in the City! Detective Swift had an advantage in working much closer to Parliament, where the MP had worked and stirred up all the conflict with his fellows who also wanted to get their draft legislation through the HoC! Man was born to compete, mused Timmon, ever since evolution had given him an intellectual brain! Press on, Aristotle; help solve a murder of national importance—Just why you were 'lent' to the Met!

Since his seconding from the Met to assist Friender, he had worked mighty hard to uncover any new facts about what involvement any locals in Hampton had had with MP Clark; a habitual visitor to the Platts. He had, using all information he had gleaned from locals, established that the MP used the Thames Island basically to leave behind the threats he suffered in Westminster for spells lasting a single day to weeks; often related to whether Parliament was sitting or in recess. He had uncovered a major clue involving two mature girls who were very close buddies and who had also been very close to MP Clark every time he visited Platt's Island. Timmon had not actually had the opportunity to meet and interview.

But the fundamental question of who had murdered the MP and why remained unsolved. It annoyed Timmon that he seemed unable to achieve the answers to these fundamental puzzles any better than his colleagues had during the main enquiry conducted soon after the MP's death. He had not found anyone holding a grudge against Clark, nor anyone who might be seeking some form of revenge. More annoying, his mates back in Westminster would happily mock him as being 'Clueless!': surely a denigration fit only for Chief Superintendents!

He was now on his way back to the City to report to an *amateur* detective who just happened to have the DCI's approval as man in charge of the case! Bah! Thank the gods he would be meeting up with DC Alan Swift, who he knew from training days and subsequent experience as junior detectives.

Friender looked forward to having a serious chat with Timmon, who had always been too busy to meet him at a location up the Thames River in the vicinity of Platt's Eyot and Tagg's Isle. What essential clues had he discovered; who did he suspect from what he'd learnt; was he holding the vital answer to who the murderer was without knowing it? In spite of Fred's territory for the repeat investigation being so environmentally idyllic, Friender had not managed to choose a better a meeting venue than his own office in Westminster!

"Sorry to drag you away from Hampton Court splendour to Westminster toil and grime, Fred. Can we get straight into your most current verdict, on what you've unearthed in the Platt's area, about the MP's murder? The private investigator felt most ego supportive taking the lead status.

"Sure! I presently reckon that although there are plenty of dubious characters in my area of investigation, only the two female suspects you previously pointed your finger at are still under suspicion as possible murderers. There's little doubt that they were intimately close to Clark and might well have become jealous of each other."

"Would that so-to-speak envy be heightened by the MP's persistent aggression towards fellow MPs over getting his draft bills through parliament and achieving official approval first, not last?" Friender raised his eyebrows in slight disrespect.

"Waste of time asking me—you're the pundit on the dead MP's office and goings on in that ball-court!" the young detective shrugged. "I'm only the junior up the river!" The PD raised both palms in accentuation of his 'out of the picture' status.

"If you've decided the two young female suspects were bosom pals, d'you consider it's at all possible that they committed the deadly act, in unison, so to speak?" The investigator cast a critically questioning look at Swift.

"I'm not here to solve any murder mystery, Sir. My DI only detailed me to find new facts where possible about all suspects in Platt's and Tagg's Islands area; mostly round the murdered MP's houseboat. I'm only there to help you, not to solve the case!"

"That's what I keep saying to myself, Fred. I'm only commissioned to find out why Clark was killed—not to find a murderer for the Met." Friender shrugged to show unity with the DC. "But once curious info begins to emerge about characters you hold in suspicion, one can't as a detective toss them onto the petty dump. Can't us two pool the info we've collected so we can reduce the suspects to one or two instead of ten to twenty!"

"Give it a try; providing you do the same with Alan Swift?"

"Done!" the ex-DCI responded.

Leaving his office, Friender was suddenly more than acutely aware of his now usual stalker. He paused to fully turn and stare at the person following him, for the first time—a female he noted with slight surprise as she, caught off guard, moved closer. He searched her face for recognisable features and was instantly shocked to realise she was one of the women he had talked to in the House of Commons. Why had she wasted so much time just following him?

He took the instant decision to challenge his stalker. "Hallo, Pearl! You fancy me so much?" He grinned at her.

"I'm makin' sure you mind yer own affairs instead o' poking yer nose where it doesn't belong!"

The investigator blew breath through narrowed lips. "Can't help doing my job, gal! That's what the fuzz's expectin' me to do. YOU know who murdered the MP?"

"Don't be stupid, how could I! He was my boss, so I want to know as much as you do. But your method of inquiry, ferreting in every corner of the House, leaves us who work there cold. As well, we don't think you're getting anywhere for all your poking and prying! Just makes us angry. You'd better watch out or one of us will cut your bleedin' ears off, as well as your nasty nose!" Pearl's eyes stared into his and her right fist clenched and rose up.

"OK, OK, I promise to back off my questioning if you swear you didn't end his life. That'd let me focus on two suspects I've firmly identified in Westminster." Friender backed away a few feet, lessening the risk of Pearl actually using her fist on him. She was no slim and short woman!

"Can I offer you a peace-pact coffee down the street? There's still a few questions I'd like to ask about MP Clark's final parliamentary act presented to the Legislative body. In particular, how many of his colleagues in the HoC were competing to get their draft Bills through the Lower House at the same time as him? That rivalry could be a motive for murder in Westminster!"

"And I could shout, 'Mind your own damn business!' But I won't because we still have to find his murderer before the whole foul business is shelved for good as insoluble by Scotland Yard. Lead me to your cup of coffee, Private Eye."

Friender was ecstatic inside about winning the dead MP's chief assistant's conceding to help him learn more about him and his competing MP colleagues. Members of the House were notoriously hard to get to give any personal info except when they themselves went before the Press to gain publicity or to further their Legislative Act quests.

Up the street in Lords' Café, with a grand size house Americano coffee in front of both parties, the frustrated investigator wasted no further vital time. "You nailed it in one, Morse! We Must find ourselves the murderer p.d.q. It means your working hero 'dies in the public eye' also. If we nail the killer, we also leave MP Clark to RIP in his grave with no tarnished image. That's one of my specialities as a PI."

The MP's secretary bent forward over the coffee table. "The MP's final Legislative Act was designed to protect ALL wildlife in any licensed park, not just the recognised species for that park. That was where one lobby contested the other's rights to claim protection. Groups in each faction were aroused enough by long-hatched differences to be capable of violent display of their hatred in public locations. I understand that you yourself ex-CID have been threatened?" The parliamentarian once again confronted him inquisitively, face to face.

Friender was delighted that her manner was no longer accusatory. "I can only repeat the question that refuses to be answered—Which of his colleagues is most likely to have wielded the knife? There must have been a more intense hatred than just an argument over drafting an Act of Parliament!"

"What about his mannerisms? You forgotten his habit of loving any and every woman he met?" She looked at him with some scorn mixed with embarrassment.

"Of course; but I try as an independent detective to look at all aspects of victims and from that to build a picture of their murderer, and hopefully from that to identify them. Envy, jealousy, contempt, rage, hatred, even fear are not personal traits of much use in identifying that particular person one hunts for. The mode of killing and the location are of far greater use as leading clues. In this particular case involving an MP, we know these factors, so finding the assassin should hypothetically follow these clear leads. That's where witnesses like you Pearl are invaluable—you knew the MP almost intimately, so you could well actually know his 'butcher' without realising it!"

"Thanks for nowt!—You gonna get one of yer DC assistants to arrest me?" She sneered.

"Waste of time, Honey—have you forgotten already; you've been crossed off the Suspect list! But I'm still waiting for you to give me the basic details on what draft Bills the MPs in your neck of the woods inside the HoC were hatching when the murder took place? If we can detail, in police verbiage, each parliamentarian's quest for public recognition, I have better hope of making out to what ends they would go and whether they still remain prime suspects."

Friender felt appalled at his own verbosity to a woman, particularly one whose job involved preparing speeches for Parliamentary presentation of legislation. Had his past dogged investigator Front been usurped by a new image of a chatterer who solved nothing in respect of unsolved cases? May even the devil forgive me, he muttered under one breath.

"That privy information is not publicly available, Tom. I cannot break the rules, even for ex-Met officers." Pearl pursed her red lips slightly.

"Boy, those days in Scotland Yard, even as a CI were a bloody site simpler than my new life is. I have to extract every clue by hammer and chisel along at Stonehenge! Can't you help a little in the hunt for your ex-boss's murderer? As I said minutes ago, you probably know the guilty party by familiarity in your job, but still refuse to let go enough info for their name to surface to one or all those investigating the case! You just have to make yourself aware that none of the rest of us 'Know' Clark's associates or friends like you do." Friender also leaned a little forward over the two coffees.

"I'm not guilty, mister—go look elsewhere instead of wasting time bothering me!" Pearl rose from the wooden chair with half back rest that fitted out the street café and walked out onto the pavement. Friender sat still; the opportunity to end his interrogation was welcome; now that the parliamentarian had proved totally uncooperative.

Basic working offices, though dreary and uninspiring, can provide a haven of rest and locus for mental recuperation. Friender was now finding his ten by eight feet work place no longer quite so inhospitable and uninspiring. A firm base in which to pause and reflect the next move was at this moment in his investigation very welcome, and relaxing enough to spawn new ideas on the immediate future for his investigation. He was uncertain if his reputation was at this stage too compromised to allow the Police DI to sanction any further investigations into the PM's murder on his part. But many years' experience in both public, as chief inspector, and Private detective toiling's cautioned his wisdom not to jump to any conclusion Yet.

'Press on,' a silent but strident voice insisted inside his brain. To review progress, he counselled himself, keep very firmly in mind that you've almost verified your diagnosis that 2+2 is no longer a speculative guess at where the murderer is located. Two suspects were located in Westminster, and two near Platt's Island up the Thames. That situation prevailing, he needed to concentrate what resources were available to himself exactly on each pair.

However, his experience warned, do not ignore other possible characters at each location, particularly men. An all-female suspects situation did not auger well for an investigator of his long experience!

The private detective opened his Notes Book to help his thinking brain revisit and recap as much as possible of the vital information he had stored in there. MP Clark had been murdered by a fatal severing of the neck jugular vein. A full police investigation had failed to identify or find the murderer. The unknown killer was still at large; could strike again. He, investigator brought in by the DI to solve the mystery, had not found the guilty party either. The dead MP's chief associate in Parliament had proved unwilling to provide basic facts regarding Clark's final legislative work in the House of Commons.

He remained certain that had a lot to do with the murder. And everyone he had encountered in the case had proved reluctant to assist in providing basic data to him. This situation left him puzzling over why. Was there a kind of 'cartel' in operation to prevent him exposing the identity of the MP's assassin. Even worse, had they 'arranged' the murder? If so, he would be forced to hand the investigation back to the Met!

Or, his common sense re-emerged, insisting he was just being over-dramatic about the case and must press on. Stop just speculating his conscience warned—find the evidence you need. That job was what he had been called in for. Forget being diverted by one and all, purposely or otherwise! Find the murderer, And their scalpel or dagger or penknife or butchers' tool. That way you'll make sure it doesn't end up slicing your neck, Investigator!

Was it obviously him at fault? Jem had pointed out to him that he, ex-CID, knew the House of Commons well, so He was expected to solve the mystery. If so, where to next? his inner conscience demanded? His memory suddenly clicked; Pearl had previously detailed a Carl, a Maisy Walsh, and a Leona Black as close associates or lovers of Clark. Which of them had he checked out in depth so far, and Where in hell in this office had he put pencilled records he'd made after any interviews he'd conducted?

Once, a while later, Friender located the required paperwork, the alarming reality hit him smack in the cerebral cortex. He'd Not actually spoken to Every single potential suspect who worked alongside the now eliminated MP! It had been early in his investigation of possible suspects working in the HoC: BUT that factor gave him minimal excuses. So, he Was at fault!

He simply must get back inside Westminster Palace, yet again, and search for members of the HoC who might have had unbearable grouses against Clark. Such a task might be monumentally difficult, not least on account of MPs being highly important persons and proving unwilling to be put through the third degree! Had his current Met inspector handed him the impossible task of unearthing the vital clues that the police detectives themselves had been unable to accomplish weeks ago?

Friender's pride, both in his past as a DCI and now as a private investigator, hassled his conscience to push aside doubt and to pursue his goal of finding MP Clark's killer. To that end, he'd jolly well force even the HoC to give up its 'skeleton in the cupboard'!

With the DI's approval and help, he made an appointment to interview the head of the HoC security guard. The Met DI was the sole one with the authority to allow a private investigator to snoop around the Palace, and to lend the assistance required.

Well inside the 12th Century spectacular architecture of the House of Commons, the investigator sat in the Head of Security's office trying to ferret out the vital information he needed to make headway with finding the murderer. Experience as a detective insisted that he Must ask only questions that might yield answers desperately needed to identify suspects. Forget the past, Friender, he silently cautioned himself, you're only finishing off work the police bungled so couldn't complete. You're Not finding and arresting any suspects you identify!

He had decided against inviting DC Alan Swift along to the interview—he would probably only confuse the basic purpose of Friender's meeting inside Parliament. Young eagerness could sometimes be a handicap, even with competent police detectives!

"Can you verify that Maisy Walsh, Leona Black and Carl are workers here who knew the late Mr Clark well on a day-to-day basis?"

"Yes." The head of security was abrupt.

"I somehow missed speaking with them on my previous visit here, or outside this Palace. What do you suggest is the least nosey, as I've been named, way of me meeting them—individually or should we arrange a get-together inside?" Friender made sure his manner was polite.

The HoS's eyelids tightened narrowly and his mouth puckered. "If you must interrupt their work to ask questions, as requested by the Met DI, I'll set up a short general meeting." The investigator was tempted to ask, "In the local pub?" but limited his reply to, "Fine, can we do that straight away?" Chances were slim he accepted, but…

"I've set up a meeting for one hour's time. A guard will accompany you outside and see you back into the House in an hour." The HoS abruptly terminated the meeting.

One hour later, as pledged, and after he had walked around the gardens for the nth time, Friender re-entered the massive entrance hall of the Palace and found himself escorted to a slightly larger meeting room. There he found the parliamentarians he sought, seated with the HoS at the head of the small table.

"These worthy people have already assured me they have no personal info on MP Clark's murder. Don't therefore, private detective, waste our combined valuable time with daft questions."

Friender was well aware that the HoS's tactic was to make him feel small. The converse was the case and he took care to pitch his interrogation cunningly "Can we start with basic evidence on the murder. Can any of you remember how your colleague died?"

"Slit vein in his neck." The answer was succinct enough to make Friender wince. These were hardened debaters in this House; not persons to be upset by tough questioning!

"And as precise as you can be, where did the grisly deed take place?" If he used harsh words, the responses should be swift and exact. Neither party had time for a chat session.

"In this House, out front in the Visitors' Entrance Great Hall, beside one of the classic statues. To pre-empt you, detective, Discovered by one of the guards."

"Thank you very much. Has anyone come across or heard of a stabbing in the neck before? I take it no one here has personal experience?" Friender expected some reaction from one or more of the occupants—it might help him build a better picture of the parliamentary group present.

Not one person seemed to even acknowledge the question. His audience just stared at him! At least, he accepted, he had one vital answer—not one of those present was a murderer. Guilt, he knew, no matter how contained, is expressed in certain fashions. But there could be MPs not coerced to this meeting who did hate Clark.

"Did anyone here object to Clark's new piece of legislature, or his methodology for pressing it through Parliament?"

The stony silence was repeated. 'What am I doing here? his logic questioned. I'm not a Chairman of committees!'

"Anyone got a bright solution for the MP's demise right here in HoC rather than back in his constituency? You're also MPs, very familiar with trudging back and forth to dual work places. What's the logic to committing the murder here? It's far trickier and concentrates suspicion more on you all." Friender spread his inverted hands over the table.

"I remind you, detective, that all present have no connection with the murder. These parliamentarians have very kindly diverted themselves from their tasks to assist you for a short time. Do not abuse such cooperation!" The HoS's reprimand was cuttingly intense rather than just rebuking.

"I need to solve the mystery of who murdered MP Clark extremely urgently; most to allow you all to relax and forget the incident. For that reason, I have had to enlist assistance from the police—The reason we are here, of course. Please lend me your combined help." Friender looked at every face, male or female, around the table.

"We understand your dilemma, investigator but none of us progress any draft legislature we propose to Parliament by murdering objectors along the way in what is a complex legal process; including many Readings in the Houses, together with Reports, Committees and final Assent, involving Her Majesty."

The speaker was a very mature woman and the investigator was well aware that she had the authority to, so-to-speak, sack him. She certainly had not been one of Clark's lovers.

"I sincerely appreciate your protest at my investigative prying into standard parliamentary procedures, Ma'am. Does anyone present know of any other parliamentarian, or outsider, who voiced strong complaints about Clark's new Act in its draft state? I suggest more than one of you might just unknowingly hold a key to the mystery. Please consider carefully!"

Another dead silence ensued. Friender remained convinced that he would uncover the vital clue here in the Palace. That lead was somehow attached to the MP's incomplete draft Act, wildlife and all; yet, how was he to discover it?

"We need to finish up, Mr Security Chief, but I also need from you a list of anyone else who was even remotely involved in drafting the Act but who's not present at this meeting. Thank you All very much for your time." Friender got up and offered a plastic smile to all participants. 'Get me back to everyday sleuthing' he muttered.

Chapter 10

He walked back down the Embankment towards Waterloo Bridge and his office, brain toiling as usual in this investigation to make any sense of seemingly incongruent events and disparate clues. MPs were almost screaming for a solving of the murder of one of them, but at the same time were following a policy of being totally unhelpful to investigators, police or private, of the death.

The murdered MP had apparently been involved with a new Act to immediately detain and where necessary punish any individual who knowingly harassed or injured a wild animal located inside one of the UK's parks; public, private or otherwise. This was likely to be hotly debated in both Houses of Parliament because of the uncertain definition of "Wild". Not all creatures in any park would be included in the proposed new Act, and this upset many members of the public, including more than a few of the dead MP's close friends and associates.

Being almost forced to act alone was nothing new to Friender, ex-policeman and now private investigator. Yet, it made no sense in this case of near National Emergency. The murderer he searched for undoubtedly had intimate knowledge of the basic objectives framed in Clark's draft new bill, and could publicise such unauthorised information tomorrow. For that reason, Parliament was behaving like a pack of wild hounds, baying for the murderer to be found and locked up. His DI boss was passing that urgency on to him relentlessly but almost refusing to help. The two young detectives were doing their best to assist on the case. But how could he, outsider, get inside the ambits of the inner HoC to question more occupants than he had done so far?

His Westminster two were virtually eliminated from any list of real suspects. Pearl, Clark's working partner, who he'd questioned in depth, was to him now free of suspicion. The other suspect woman also had been cleared at the HoC meeting he'd just finished. The other two of his 2+2, Platt's and Tagg's Islands or Hampton girls, had also been virtually cleared of murder—he cautioned himself that he must absolutely verify that fact—a final revisit up the Thames!

Hell, this case had required more journeying back and forth than any other he could recall! The repayment account he would have to submit to the Met by the end of the case would be hefty!

He paused on his walk past the public entrance to the lofty lobby of the near century old HoC just to rethink the murder once more. Victim's corpse dragged in and dumped beside one of statues, just out of full and immediate public view. No blood left, so the police coroner had to analyse death in an unknown location. Two cleaner ladies had reported moving the body out of full view because they had assumed the person was drunk. No member of the public had reported any other suspicious activity. The case remained a mystery to this day!

Friender returned to the exact location inside the lobby where the corpse had been found and examined. If it had been moved, as reported, where exactly had it been dumped by the murderer initially? He slowly and meticulously retraced the pathway of the victim to the best of his knowledge. Beside the Gladstone Statue, just out of instant sight to all members of the visiting public. Was the body conveyed over the shoulder or in some receptacle? The first would have meant dumping it onto the chequered tile floor. The alternative would have involved some way of unobvious offloading, maybe around a corner behind been the statue of Churchill.

With his analytical mind in speedy-answers mode, the investigator deduced that it would not have been unbeatably tough to pull the dead body, encased in an appropriate sack, across the entrance lobby floor to the selected drop-off point. That made it more plausible that the murder had taken place well outside the HoC. And it also tallied with the guilty party being from some other location of work. BUT, Friedman halted his brain from drawing more false assumptions; such a delusion would be exactly what the committer of the crime wanted!

Overtaken with conflicting clues about the murderer, the investigator halted any further searching inside the HoC. He remained almost convinced that the corridors of legislative power were the obvious working location for a likely murderer. Yet, without contestable evidence, he had to resume his poking around for stronger clues elsewhere. And that now somehow whiffed of River. The Thames had dominated this case from the beginning of his involvement and now needed deeper exploration of how it might fit into his understanding of events up to the stabbing. Could the Major Canal supplying the Capitol be somehow used to kill? There were 45 locks, any of which could have been used to drown the victim. The neck slitting could have been post mortem; to confuse those who found the MP's body in the lobby of the House of Commons. The Mystery deepened with every new clue he unearthed!

Before starting any new odyssey of investigation into exactly where the murderer had vanished to, Friender contacted his up-river DC colleague, Fred Timmon.

"Any news, ace detective? Don't put your magnifying glass or your curiosity to rest yet, Fred. We may have almost searched every rivulet, boat yard and house boat on Platt's Ait and Tagg's Isle but let's not give up searching for that elusive lead hidden somewhere on the Isle. I'm not being hypercritical if I remark that Met tends to cease their investigations as soon as they've zilch evidence of any way forward. With far less stacked against me, that's my trick for triumphing against pretty bad odds—stick with it!"

"You're to be admired, Super-sleuth. How will continuing to rummage around one unrewarding island help us? You're the Genius—so give me the lead we all seek!" Friender almost sensed over the phone the PD's impatience with no progress.

"Have you explored the locks up-river? They'd make ideal locations to murder someone. Maybe wherever there is one, the loch-keeper just might recollect noting something odd!"

"Good thinking, Mr Friender. I've just had a flash recall, by the way, are you savvy with a woman named Leona Black? Apparently she visited the MP up here in Hampton quite often." The police detective's voice expressed guarded but definite interest in the clue he'd discovered.

"My answer is Yes. I've come across her quite a few times down here in Westminster. Her joining with Clark occurred some time ago. Quite how close they were I'm not sure of. I'm not in the knowhow either as to why she would have met him in the area of Platt's when he had dozens of female admirers down here in parliament. But if we understood killers and victims closely in every case we tackled Fred, we'd have no challenges in our jobs as detectives, of any variety!"

Friender chatted easily on his mobile with his Thames River Islands PD helper, even though his now hyperactive mind was way elsewhere working out the quickest course to interrogating the HoC group of parliamentarians again. He just had to gain deeper facts about this Leona Black woman, pdq. Was she a buddy of Pearl's, or did she belong to a separate parliamentary set?

Much as he had no liking for his temporary work office, he remained pleased that it was situated only a short walking distance from the HoC. He tried to keep walking near home, to maintain some level of fitness. His working life in the Met had been pretty active exercise-wise and he had strived to keep some degree of vigour since retiring. He knew it helped maintain synaptic workings in his brain, vital to being a first-class investigator.

To complete his first round of data exchange with PD colleagues now working on the case of the murdered MP, Friender once again telephoned Alan Swift, his co-worker in Westminster. "I've just spoken to Fred about the search and question task he's responsible for up the River in the Hampton area. He's been on and off Platt's Ait like a ferret looking for a weasel meal and has questioned dozens of people living or working there. We've uncovered a few minor suspects but, lamentably, no murderer as yet."

"I've been talking yet again to the parliamentarians you pointed out to me, but I too still have no concrete suspects who fit the image of a killer." The PD's voice was close to being discouraged; almost enough to give up the hunt.

"As I advised Fred, don't give up searching for that elusive lead hidden somewhere in the House of Commons, Alan. I may be hypercritical if I accuse the Met of tending to abandon their investigations as soon as they've zilch evidence of any way forward. So stick with it, Alan! We can win."

The investigator felt pleased that his contacts with the two police detectives seconded to him from the Met was improving, and that progress with screening the public at Westminster and Platt's was also improving on the unsatisfactory results he had managed to achieve previously on his own. He had, he rebuked himself, almost forgotten what a success teamwork could be! He after all was in charge and his basic skill as a good solver of unanswered murder mysteries was what the police chief recognised.

In his investigator experience, the desperado, as he liked to classify the murderer, was still located in the HoC. Clever operators committed the foulest offences in the territory with which they were most familiar. There they were least likely to be noticed acting out of character or illegally. There they also went unnoticed in the day, even if acting slightly oddly. There was much less protocol these days and men behaving strangely was almost 'The Norm'.

And that was where clever investigators like him scored success; re-examine perpetrators or revisit scenes of crime using skilled interrogation and fine-tuned probing techniques. His style of refusing to surrender to instant, unrewarding solutions to unsolved crimes. He'd soon earnt in his early days with the Met that failure was tantamount to Useless!

The voice in his head insisted, "Bite the bullet, Friender, and press on! You've a case of death by foul deed to unravel and resolve. You'll need police help for that."

The private investigator sat by himself on one of the benches upfront in the windowed cabin of a Thames river cruiser, heading west upstream. He had always been amazed by the sheer power of the river's current beneath—sufficient in inclement weather to turn the sizeable ferry boat over and drag it downstream; to fatal consequences of any passengers, and crew!

Such perils were of no concern to Friender at this moment. His thoughts were yet again focused absolutely on finding MP Clark's killer, pretty quick if he was to preclude the House of Commons exploding from the reported warring factions in its depths. The dead MP had basically done no more than introduce a plan to protect the Wildlife in Parks, but it must have been his modus operandi that fired up the war of words that had become heated enough to result in his own murder. Who, he questioned himself riding up the Thames, could have hated enough to use a razor-sharp knife to vertically slit the MP's jugular vein? Just the mental picture of the victim collapsing from such a spurting loss of blood made him stop thinking and just watch the river water approaching, then splashing noisily past the bow.

If, as evidence confirmed, MP Clark had taken time off parliament to explore up the Thames and canals beyond the head, he must have visited most of the islands or aits many times. Where, in addition to Platt's or Tagg's, would have been the ideal location for the murderer to have met or lured him? In addition to all his current investigative work, he must go back towards Westminster and explore the smaller islands downstream for a potential heavily wooded location ideal for killing someone unseen. The prospect of such a gruesome event triggered the sensation of nausea he had experienced many times lately, fortifying his strong belief that he should never have taken on investigating a brutal murder, even though he'd gone into some sickening crimes in his time in the Met!

He'd gone back to the police senior inspector in charge of the murder enquiry. "Stan, I'm in a dilemma. Sorry to trouble you once again. Do you exactly know who the two factions in the HoC were that got so fired up about MP Clark's proposed new Act of Parliament? If you can help me by filling in the basic facts of the case that I'm struggling with, I'm sure I'll be better able to provide you, the police, with the answers you desperately want about the murderer."

"I thought you'd questioned All the MP's staff and co-workers about the draft document, and who any antagonists were?" The DI's tone was sharp as always.

"OK, Stan, but did you fully comprehend why two factions developed over the wording Wild Life in the draft, in the first place? Such a difference of opinion amongst those who'd read the draft wouldn't surely be enough to provoke murder?" Friender's face furrowed to convey his disbelief.

"I've no idea Friender! I'm a Detective Inspector not a mind reader or philosopher. I'd say, impromptu, that political causes had nothing to do with it. I always assumed the murder had a personality basis. Someone was tormented by MP Clark's intentions enough to make them determined to put a stop to him!

"On that, we're in absolute agreement. That makes my mission a damned sight simpler. I'm investigating a Person driven mad by Clark, Not by his obsession with animals in parks. I suggest to you that we're searching for an Outsider to the central issue we've all focused on so far. As in so many classic murder enquiries, we've omitted the butler and chambermaid, manager or advisor, unrewarded supporter and star follower. I've clearly got a lot more people in the background of HoC to interrogate and look into. Thankyou DI; you've been mighty helpful, yet again."

The private investigator left New Scotland Yard and drove to a parking space outside the HoC. He raised one hand to the guard as he walked through the entrance lobby to one of the corridors beyond. He had already deduced two options for questioning; the murdered MP's secretary, now moved on, or Carl, the long-term associate.

Now accomplished in finding a way around HoC, he used a quickly scribbled list of contacts to begin a search for parliamentarians that he had overlooked previously in his quest for a likely suspect murderer. This time he realised that no political establishment stone must be left unturned or legislative assistant neglected in the new investigation. Unveiling further clues and persuading every interviewee to provide vital data would yield the identity of the killer he wanted—now more urgently than ever!

He felt relieved by the certainty that one DI and two PD's would swiftly deal with any suspect He managed to identify. It provided the professional clout to find and question additional parliamentarians who he had not yet tackled. Somewhere in here, under one of the tallest square towers in the world, a murderer was waiting for likely exposure. He, now the chief searcher, had the responsibility to achieve just that—expose the MP's murderer. The word sent a cold chill up his neck. That person might kill again any time! Around a corner in this historic edifice could lie a razor-sharp knife in a manic hand, waiting to slice his jugular from top to bottom! And, there were no police here to swiftly prevent it happening.

Friender sat down for several minutes to think. He had undertaken more nerve shattering investigations while with the Met but was it intelligent for him to be pushing his Investigational luck in these corridors of hidden power? And, you just exposed a fresh clue without thinking, Tom! To use a sharp blade with such expertise meant professional training. So, the murderer, whether they worked in the HoC or not, had cutting skills learnt elsewhere; apprentice butcher, surgeon, abattoir worker, pathology dissector? Yet, more very personal questions to ask everyone he interrogated here on!

After he had tracked down and talked with many of the potential suspects on his revised list, the private investigator had vacated the Commons once again; to pursue his enquiries in more unassuming locations in the City of Westminster. He walked to the embankment of the Thames, to yet again scour the location for fresh ideas rather than clues *per se*. At first glance the mighty river's waters surging past with might and persistence offered but fleeting inklings of a human life destroyed.

Who would follow a MP from the HoC to the riverside and how then to murder them, right here under his feet? And then drag the body back to the House and dump it! "Steady, Tom!" he cautioned his momentarily over-active mental senses. "Deal with each element of the enigma one atom at a time!"

The simplest answer to his first mental query was "NOBODY!"

The murderous act must have been carried out in an isolated location Upstream. Because downstream there were no river islands. Friender was assuming that murder committed outside had to be done masked by some form of vegetation. What more likely place than amongst trees in a wood; the size of it immaterial? But there was little of that sort of vegetation on the river except on one of the few islands located, or built by dumping reservoir excavations, Upstream!

Must he go back yet again towards the head of Old Father Thames' Canal to find the real murder site—the scene where MP Clark's corpse had been dumped inside a floating coffin to be swept down to Westminster bridge? His brain almost screamed that there had to be a more mystery-solving tactic to employ. He was, he calmly assured his mind, cleverer as an investigator than simple grovelling about on river banks!

The obvious alternative of searching yet again along some four kilometres of corridors spreading out from the Lobby at the centre of the House of Commons or Westminster Hall for the murder suspect was equally as daunting. But in that very centuries-old architectural complex hid the guilty party he sought. And He, Tom Friender private Investigator, was Not going to be prevented from achieving his contracted task, even if he singly was doing the detective work that the Met should have completed weeks ago!

They lay in waiting for the private investigator in the small park outside his office building. It frustrated them that they actually worked inside the HoC but could not risk accosting him inside for fear of being caught. That circumstance would immediately destroy the deep longing they all felt for an end to being hunted for the MP's murder. They strongly felt that He had deserved being executed, for multiple wrongdoings in preparations of legislative Acts; all involved with wildlife living in countryside and parks.

Friender approached his office building vigilantly. He had been threatened, so being sharply aware of one's surroundings and anyone in them who looked suspicious was vital to survival. He therefore spotted a likely assailant long before they leapt out at him, so to speak. The camouflaged woman approached with clear intent once she realised that Friender had picked her out.

"I warned you to leave us alone, Nosey-parker! Go back upstairs to your office and read your comics and mags, and leave us hard working parliamentarians to get on!"

"Queen and Country, and all that!" the investigator responded. "Problem is at the moment all your good at is killing your own MPs. If you'd help us to sort out who murdered your close workmate Clark, then we'd leave you House of Commons rabbits in peace in your trendy burrows hidden inside the Palace." Friender shook his head to emphasise his criticism.

"We can solve House of Commons problems ourselves, Mister Snoop!" Her hands rested firmly on her hips in defiance.

"You and who? You've failed so far with the Metropolitan Police! That's precisely why I'm on the case! Care to assist me?" The Investigator widened his eyes to heighten his demand.

"We know it was done outside, so what good is there to offering to help you keep snouting around inside the House, our territory?" The parliamentarian's voice was heavily poisoned with sickly scorn.

Friender paused to weigh her assertion of innocence. How did she know that Clark must have been murdered further up the Thames? Only he and DC Swift possessed that information, so this would-be intimidator suddenly ranked high on the suspect list! Did she know the murderer OR was she familiar with the dead MP's real ambitions in Parliament?

He could ask his inspector boss to apprehend and question her but the Met would have done that already and she would only 'clam up' once again, giving nothing away. That put the onus firmly back on him to return to ferreting into Clark's department personnel for the murderer!

"Sorry, I don't think I got your name?"

"That's my personal business! I worked with Clark but I didn't murder him. And I haven't the foggiest idea who did. Get back in your damn office and leave us alone!"

"Tell you what," the investigator had felt a sudden brain-flash, "You lot in the House of Commons have got a major public scandal to cover up! St Stephen would cringe in horror!"

"I wouldn't know; I'm an innocent bystander." The camouflaged woman almost sneered at him.

Friender recognised, from a long working life of questioning suspicious persons as detective and then investigator, that claims of innocence meant sure guilt. But of what? Familiarity with the status of Clark's typical MP's fiddling with parliamentary draft legislation? Or being involved with exchanging information, not yet public, with parliament's dealers? Or knowing details of the murder she wasn't willing to expose?

"You still got access to the MP's draft Acts, because I'm building a strong hunch that We'll find the vital clue in there." He had accentuated the 'W' to try to draw her closer to accepting him as a working colleague.

"Wouldn't know a vital clue if I slept with it. I gather you've got official permission to explore the House but you do your own sleuthing. Don't expect any help from me."

Friender had recognised her voice several minutes ago. "Selene, if you persist with your apparent reluctance to assist me, and that includes the Met force detailed to solving the MP's foul murder, I'll be forced to re-instate you as the main murderer suspect. That, I must stress, I don't want because it'll set us back weeks!"

"Good, snoops like you need to be helped as little as possible! I've warned you to lay off bothering us in the House of Commons, so I'm off, as far away from you as possible!"

Friender walked out of the magnificently designed, now historic lobby entrance to the HoC. He remained irritated, if not disillusioned, by his inability to evaluate any progress made at each step of an investigation. He was used to sitting down and analysing each day's developments after work. But being involved in a murder mystery of such National importance changed the rules of questioning if he wanted to make any advances of some worth in solving the case. In frustration he sought-out the closest park bench and sat down with paper and pencil, retrieved seconds ago from his trouser pocket.

First advance, he had identified two possible murder suspects at two locations, Westminster and Hampton on Thames. His long-trained enquiring mind still pigeonholed these as his 2+2mayBe.

Second, although MP Clark had undoubtedly been murdered inside the HoC, exactly why remained unresolved. The killer had to be exposed to answer this enigma.

Was even he, well-recognised sleuth, unsuited to the task set for him by the failed police force investigating the MP's death?

Yet he had not, as of this moment, actually failed his old colleague, the detective chief inspector in charge of the case!

So, he admonished himself, Friender pick up the shards of data you've amassed so far and do your well-known detective trick of establishing who the actual killer is! You were called in to help, so do so pronto before the murderer strikes again, or think on it, gets you!"

Chapter 11

The first still unresolved question he had to sort out was precisely why? MP Clark had been murdered. The case inspector had invited his help pretty late on, well after the police investigation had been virtually closed. But he, private investigator, now had on hand a mass of data on the murder victim's parliamentary work, House of Commons office, working colleagues, and other facts relating to his real character, modus operandi and final hours alive. But, until the why was resolved, there was little hope of identifying that killer!

Friender had not been anywhere near the House of Commons office at the time when it witnessed the MP's fatal stabbing down the jugular vein in his neck. He had obtained some basic information about the MP's hard work to progress his Bill on Wildlife in Parks from the MI5 squad on the case. Yet, the exact basis for murdering the poor chap inside the House and them dumping the body in the Entrance Lobby on public display was still mighty far from clear.

For that reason, he had been 'called in' to help solve the murder mystery and find the killer. Re-scrutinising all the terse scribbles in his notepad, he knew the only way forward was to go back into the HoC. He still had the senior inspector's approval to ferret inside the offices where the dead MP had researched and composed his new Act of Parliament, for that vital clue Everyone sought in order to find the assassin.

That offensive colleague of Clark's would be no help, but this time he intended to use another route of investigation into the original design, preliminary writing and subsequent progress of the Draft Act. Personal experience in digging for real facts in unsolved murders had taught him to revisit and reanalyse All the facts in unresolved cases. The brain was a truly remarkable organ of intellectual enquiry if and when utilised fully to understand and interpret data that streamed through its nerve pathways.

Friender nodded his head and smiled at the guards stationed in the intricately tiled HoC entrance, on his way through the Central Lobby, the core of the historic Palace of Westminster. Moving on down a quite narrow corridor, he relocated Clark's old office, not a star chamber to match either House of Parliament yet the place where the MP had met his end.

"Apologies for intruding yet again, Miss," he drew the attention of the office girl seated behind one of the small desks. "I'm still keen to obtain a few final details of Mr Clark's untimely demise in here." He accentuated the final two words to force her attention.

"I'm not here to answer questions from nosy intruders! But if it'll get rid of you once and for all, I'm prepared to help for a few minutes. Where's your starting point?" She looked straight at him, not too disapprovingly this time.

"We know basically that the MP was fighting a verbal battle with opponents to his new Bill to immediately detain and where necessary punish any individual who knowingly harassed or injured a wild animal found inside one of the UK's protected parks. Strike a bell?" The investigator smiled encouragingly.

"Since the Act remains incomplete, that was his business not yours to interfere with!" The responsive look on the girl's face had dissipated.

"Steady on, Miss, you've no reason to brand me as interfering! I remind you that the whole of Parliament still awaits us finding the murderer and putting them behind bars. Murder is a criminal offence, Miss, and between us we Must assist the police. I'm convinced the vital clue lies in this office, being closely tied up with a mystery someone here who is radically opposed to Clark's obsession with protecting wild life."

"There's no one here that stupid to murder for the sake of an Act of Parliament!" She sneered.

"You're way off-beam I'm afraid. Murders have taken place in Parliament since five centuries ago!" Friender resisted the temptation to wag a reprimanding finger at the girl. He happened to have a personal interest in British history, initially inspired by what he had learnt at school.

"There must be written or online accounts of actions, discussions and progress made in the drafting of Clark's proposed Act? If you've not been in this office long, d'you have any idea where the Old office's accounts or proceedings are now?" The Investigator felt in his historical element delving into all facts surrounding an unsolved murder case. He had loved his career in the Met; but facts and figures tended to be served up on an official plate, to be dealt with in proper rotation. Now he was unrestricted in how he did his detective work, each new clue seemed a real challenge on its own, uncluttered by officialdom and bureaucracy.

"Diaries are on those shelves across there." The office girl waived one hand at the shelving behind Friender. "But, even policemen need approval to delve into House of Commons official records. This isn't a public library, you know!" He sensed her almost spit the scorn she felt at him.

"I have that authorisation from the Speaker. Can you help me find any records for the day of the murder? I want out of here as much as you seem to wish me out! Help me identify the felon and the House'll be able to relax." Friender outstretched his hands to her.

"Alright, alright." The girl stood up and reached for a handful of records off the shelf. "You know the date." She handed him the soft-bound books. "I've got work to do for Parliament, so you find your killer. That's your job!"

Friender, mindful that he was straying inside HoC official territory, set about finding any helpful entries as swiftly as he could. On the actual day of Clark's brutal death there were strangely few records of visitors to the office. The MP had apparently left his office on a pre-arranged visit to Platts Eyot, near Hampton, up the Thames. That did not make any sense, his brain insisted. Clark adored his female friends but his every attention in his last hours would have been focussed on getting his draft Bill through Parliament sitting at the time.

Yet, he at once analysed, that event would account for there being no blood found in the vicinity of the corpse; as reported in the post mortem and pointed out to him by his inspector. The body discovered in the Lobby had originated from elsewhere. But why would the murderer have gone through such an elaborate ritual to end the MP's life and terminate his function as an MP? If he could answer that, hey presto the identity of one, or more, murderers should be revealed.

He had been up the famed river several times; though nowhere like the number of times or 215 miles' distance that Clark had, as part of his Canals & Waterways hobby. Was it really necessary for him to go up to Hampton Court Palace and visit the Eyot up-river yet again? Pretty much just to check out the dead MP's fancy life once more! The two women he'd identified as possible suspects up there were no longer of concern—he'd 'cleared' them from his list of possible murderers. He had also put to bed the two women that he had identified here in the vicinity of the HoC early on. His strong interrogations over the past two weeks, with help from DC Alan Swift, had satisfied him that they were innocent.

At this point in his own inquiry, the private investigator caustically labelled his own performance as Mediocre—certainly no improvement on the Met squad he had been contracted in by the detective inspector to replace; and to succeed in identifying the murderer still at loose.

'Press on, Diehard,' the investigator muttered to himself. 'Your reputation is founded on your ability to assemble the facts in an unsolved murder in such a way as to expose likely suspects missed by others. This one's the toughest yet but the Top Dog, Parliament, has called *you* in. So, straighten your ex-police cap and find the answer to who, why and how murdered no less a person than an MP. The Inspector says the whole Country wants the answer—so give it to them—win, win and quick, quick!'

He struck his forehead lightly with a fist to bring himself back to reality. "You any idea exactly who the persons recorded in this diary would be?" he turned back to the office girl.

"I said I'd help, so needs must I suppose!" She walked over to stand beside him and to glare at the open pages. "Inspector of Parks, HoC accounts person, friend of the MP, an office worker from another corridor, and an office renovation engineer. Satisfied?"

"Thank you. What if a person who works here in HoC came in—would any record be made? I understand that many an MP had viewed the draft wording in between 'Readings', and then promptly disagreed with the proposed Act."

He had not worked in a multi-manned busy office for years, BUT his intuition sounded an alarm in his mind about the likelihood of an intern as main murder suspect. Contest for performance or recorded positive outcomes was often fiercest 'in-house'. With knives becoming so to speak 'at large in the City; indeed almost *popular* at the present, murder as an act of vengeance was not so uncommon. Since Westminster Palace covered eight acres and contained at least eight kilometres of passageways, there was no way of estimating how many persons had access to the dead MP's office. Coorh! Was there really any chance of identifying the murderer in this veritable maze of officialdom?

"I'm surprised you're allowed to work in here alone with the murderer still at large!" Friender looked at the secretary sympathetically. "If what they killed for is still in here, you should be safeguarded by company." He stopped himself mocking her. "But I'm here to find evidence not to lecture you."

"You're sure, right there! Anyone has the right to visit here, why else is it called the Commons? Even the Lords can visit!" She turned over a page. "You expecting the perpetrator to have signed this diary in capitals and red ink?"

Friender was finding the office girl's reaction to his simple questioning verging on inflammatory. She was a hard adversary to get to cooperate. "Sorry to keep questioning—do you yourself have particular buddies who visit this office?"

"Remember? I don't normally work here!"

He could no longer cope with her arrogant rejection of his justified presence in the PM's office. "Thanks! I'll just keep looking for the vital clues the police need in their hunt for the murderer. You carry on—pretend I'm not here."

"What'd anyone want to murder Mr Clark for? Makes no sense—he was only doing his job! And I can't understand why the police are just bungling along." She almost snorted.

Friender chose to ignore the girl's haranguing and concentrated his total attention on finding who was in or visited the office on the fatal day. Had the MP gone alone up the Thames? Or had someone enticed him elsewhere to end his life? Why the elaborate charade, ending with dumping the body in the entrance Lobby upstairs? Who had despised the MP that much? Was a determination to champion protection of wildlife enough cause to 'drive another person to commit murder'?

He suddenly realised that his whole mind was scrambled with too many riddles to proceed with his investigation any further just at this moment.

"I feel in need of a rest from bookwork for a few minutes. Care to join me for a tea or coffee in the café?" He smiled at the office girl. "What's your name, by the way?"

"Cath, short for Catherine. 'Spose a free cuppa is too hard to turn down, even with a stranger who's meddling in your office." She did not reciprocate with any smile.

Ten minutes later, he was still questioning the girl, but now over a cup of coffee and a bun in a café in Westminster Road. "You had a chat with any of Clark's old working friends that you can recall? We need that final clue to expose the guilty party and I'm mighty hopeful you and me can find it."

"How many times?—I'm NOT a detective!" Cath almost shouted at him.

"OK, OK!" He changed his topic of chat. "You enjoy working in the House? Is it an Interesting sort of occupation? My time in the Met was often intriguing but you're so to speak right at the central heart of the Government of England." Friender broadened his eyebrows and smiled to inspire her to talk a little longer.

"I like it. But I hate working under the threat of a murder all around. Where's the one who did it?" For the first time her face softened into an 'Aid me with sympathy' mode.

"That's what we're going to find out. You and me can find the vital clue; right here in your HoC office if we work at it." He smiled encouragingly. "There's no better place for a perpetrator to hide than right where they committed the nasty act—scene of crime. For a start, can we find who might have disagreed with Clark's draught Act? Could the murderer just be one of those who was most ardently against the MP's wording and meaning of Wildlife?"

Friender had just begun to realise what an enigma MP Clark's murder really was—the killer must have been driven by an opposing combination of anger and dire necessity to shroud events in a haze of mystery. Was one of Clark's associates either obsessed with a correct definition of 'Wildlife' or afraid of being exposed for lethally challenging the new act, or just livid with Clark's success in progressing his draft bill?

He renewed his efforts to find the paperwork in this office that contained the ultimate clue; either a competing draft Act being put through parliament by another MP or Clark's own records of trips to any of the myriad of islands in the Thames other than Platt's Ait, or any other clerical work that signified loathing for Clark or scribbled plans to end his life. He was unable to escape from the conviction that he was close to uncovering the vital clue but Not quite there yet.

'Wait a moment' his brain shouted; 'you've forgotten yet again the two DC's! He was on his mobile before the reminder inside his skull had calmed down. "Alan; I need you here in the HoC office. How long?"

"Long time no-see! I'll be there forty-five minutes—Oh, I've got some new info for you. I'll be there'"

Friender put away the mobile and returned to ploughing through yet more diary paperwork, to fill in time rather than satisfy any curiosity. He was a seasoned investigator and usually realised when a particular mass of data was unlikely to yield further clues to a murder; the reason he had called-in the police this time. Just ploughing through old data was not his choice as the quickest route to exposing any murderer.

"So what new line of questioning are you proposing to send me on?" Alan Swift, DC spoke into Friender's ear.

"Ah; you made good time DC. I'd like you to take over this search through HoC records because you're far better at it than me; also being a 'man of law' gives you access to many files that I've no authority to examine. Since you've been here before, you'll be familiar with the maze of storage below this office. Can you find any vital clues of double-dealing by Clark himself, under the guise of 'Parliament'? Alternatively, have there been malicious threats to the MP by members of the public, resulting in his death by one of them?"

"Lead me on, Tom." DC Swift grinned benignly. He had sorted and analysed records available in Westminster pertinent to MP Clark's murder, and seemed to himself to have interviewed hundreds of people over only a very few days. Without unearthing the vital clue so many investigators avidly sought, he was no more savvy than they!

He had not worked on a principal murder investigation before; so was mighty keen to make his mark as a first-class DC during this official search for the assassin; of no less than a Member of Parliament.

"You're the detective, Alan! Let's start by summarising the findings so far of what's been a very prolonged police search. I'll try not to bore you; MP Clark was killed by a stabbing of the neck, he died elsewhere from here, the HoC, but his body was dumped out in the open in the entrance Lobby, MI5 still has no clue to the murderer, and Parliament remains very unhappy about the state of affairs."

Friender paused. Other than utilising the DC to fish-out records he himself was not allowed to access, was there anything his police co-worker might be able to do that he, private investigator, could not? He felt his brain buzzing with anticipation of finding an answer—there had to be Something!

"When you interviewed other MPs did anyone seem overcritical of Clark's draft Bill? Did you find any very strong supporters of the lobby campaigning to leave wildlife in

England's Parks alone? Did you manage to interrogate anyone from the Lake District; England's largest Park?"

"Wooh! I'm not Superman, Tom. There are of course objectors to the Draft; I expect there always are to any new Bill. If I see correctly where you're coming from, then NO! I found no-one who needs to be questioned further about any intent to murder!" The DC's face puckered as he grimaced to show his disgust as a professional at being himself questioned by a private detective.

"But I think we need to go back again through all the data we've amassed, one paragraph step by step, searching for those leads that the police squad overlooked previously." Friender shrugged. "It's only human to miss crucial pointers during the initial dissection of any murder. We've been given the task of probing a second time for clues missed the first time. So, let's do just that. Put your thinking cap on and go back mentally through all the individual characters you came across. Ask yourself if any one of them stood out as *odd* or Not to be trusted? This office is ours to use, so take your time recollecting."

Friender emphatically disliked lecturing the DC but they desperately needed that vital clue.

"Did Anybody seem angry about being discarded from the MP's sexy list? Was anyone connected with the meat trade, skilled with knives or cutting tools? Anyone in direct rivalry for getting their Draft through Parliament First?" His brain absolved into temporary confusion at his own goading quest for answers.

"Plenty of women a bit spiteful about being *dropped* but no-one seemed murderous in their responses to my questioning. How's about other MPs you questioned?" The DC's shrewd eyes searched into the depths of Friender's own. "Anyone absolutely fuming about Clark's good progress with his draft Act through standard Parliamentary procedures?"

"At most some annoyance. I think I've chosen the wrong tactic for us to employ, Alan—apologies! We might be better looking closely at any other draught Acts actually being put through this office of the murdered MP Clark."

His mobile phone rang in his pocket. Retrieving it he pressed the speak key. "Hallo, Friender here."

"Tom. This is Chief Inspector from the Met. Are you making Any headway with the MP's murder case? I'm getting senior MPs on my back, more and more about Parliament being kept waiting for results. Have you identified the murderer yet?" His voice was acidic and hypercritical to say the least.

But having been in the Met a while back, the investigator was long used to the surreal urgency of hierarchy. He needed to reply with sufficient confidence to mollify his temporary supervisor.

"All in-hand, Chief. We've checked-out all personnel here who might have held malicious grievance against MP Clark. No suspects there, to our knowledge. We've now turned to re-examining all documentation in Clark's office for any vital clues as to why someone might have motive or need to remove the MP in order to expedite their own paperwork through the House." The investigator paused to allow his supervisor to voice approval, or otherwise.

"Sounds like you're still fishing in the dark! Speed it up or the HoC may put you in the dock."

Friender hesitated to reply in defence since the House needed an answer to *who*, not more excuses from him.

"Done, Sir." He cut off his mobile and turned back to DC Swift. "We're being castigated by your chief for lack of a named assassin. We'd best sort through all these documents once again and find a logical cause or an identity for the murderer. Otherwise, we are the ones *on the block*." He shrugged in camaraderie style.

"Know what," the DC chatted. "We've forgotten the Thames and linked canals, where the MP was murdered, on an island made centuries ago of dumped reservoir construction diggings. We need to look for any reference to Canal & Waterways Trust, which our dead MP belonged to, in case there's any hint of Clark meddling with that institute's administration, as well as that of Wildlife protection." Alan puckered his lips.

"That would certainly spread the net of possible persons, including MPs, with heartfelt anger against Clark! But, Alan, we must *first* discover in all this paperwork a lead to Which draft Act so infuriated the killer or killers. Was Clark working on it at the moment of his murder or did it date back like a time festering sore?"

Friender felt no objection to the DC assuming control at this point—Alan had much easier access to manpower assistance than he did. A reminder, his conscious jolted him, that he must contact the DC upstream about any new clues from Platt's Eyot or Tagg's island. He had discounted the two suspects that he had interviewed up there; But it could be disastrous to finding the killer if he neglected that the vital clue might still lurk outside the City Westminster zone, way-away from the HoC after all!

They searched onerously yet again through all the office records and diaries. Neither enjoyed doing basic office work—they were detectives!

"This lot isn't of course official documentation of Acts of Parliament." DC Swift observed.

"Quite, Alan, but don't lose sight of our new quest for hidden clues that were missed by all before us."

"I'm not so sure the excitement won't give me a heart attack! Murder Mysteries are not our bread-and-butter in the Met. Hang-on! There's an entry in this diary that refers to a planned meeting between the MP and someone who's voiced an objection to his misrepresentation in the draft legislation of what constitutes 'wildlife' in parks."

"Sounds very promising to me!" Friender could barely keep excitement out of his response. He no longer worked on murder cases in a team so felt an internal thrill at making a major advance; not on his own in this one. "Any name?"

"Leona Black." She's detailed as another MP's assistant. "Department of Rural Affairs is mentioned below the name." DC Swift displayed no noticeable enthusiasm; he had worked on many suspect murder investigations—although not previously on the murder of a MP!

"You should have lived centuries ago—MPs were knocked-off with monotonous regularity! Enough banter; can you check on Leona? Your phone may be enough to get the full low-down from your department? We need to move! HoC officers knocking on the doors at the Yard will more than stir up a hornet's nest of your Senior Chiefs!"

"Tell you what, Alan," he continued. "If 'our MP' hadn't been murdered in such a grizzly display fashion, we'd not be under such intense hassle to resolve the case. Being sliced down the neck and dumped in the Lobby, front of the House, was too emotionally hurtful an ending to life for most parliamentarians. No wonder we're under such pressure!" Friender grimaced and shook his head in disgust at the images in his own mind.

"Let's just press on! If I follow up on main suspect Leona Black, can I leave you check-out the remainder of the diary entries in here, the MP's office?" The DC asked the independent.

"Not a task I'm used to or very expert at, but Yes I will. It's just possible a bumbling ex-senior detective might stumble across the clue purely by mistake. I haven't the foggiest what I'm looking for, so that raises the chances of a Class *A* stumble. Boy will we be glad to move on from mundane office data and begin looking for a named perpetrator in person! Press on, McSwift!"

Friender returned to his own persistent quest, looking for the unknown. To an extent it was easier looking for the I-don't-know-what because the mind could focus more astutely on spotting any oddities in the diary entries and notes. He was well aware from long experience in investigational practice that almost Every individual person wrote notes or recorded events in different ways and very varied styles. Yet, clues in the wordage that related to a major theft, rape or murder invariably stood out from the written text, almost as flashing beacons of criminality.

"Any more on your Black suspect? I haven't yet found much in these office diaries that might relate to intent to murder the *MP for Wildlife*." Friender glanced up at the DC hopefully. He despised paperwork. 'Give us a lead,' he mentally implored the file at hand.

"I think we owe her as an MP's chief assistant more than just 'Black suspect'! Leona has a degree and is well regarded as an expert in her work representing parliament in the wildlife parks. She does have experience in post-mortem examinations of dead wildlife but no history of being confrontational or threatening towards other humans. She will have wielded a knife many times but has shown no recorded aggression towards friend or foe.

"Point taken. Any fresh ideas on where we might proceed to from here on? We don't, in spite of a heap of skills as gumshoes, appear to have the enquiry skills to pick up any significant pointers to the murderer right here at the scene of this crime!" Friender glanced around at the veritable fortress of data they were battling to penetrate. Cath, being its keeper, might well know a way around it, but he was stymied.

"I thought you insisted that the MP was actually murdered Upstream on the Thames, in a canal or lock? Shouldn't we re-examine the river islands once again rather than dig and delve here in the HoC?" DC Swift's voice now had an exasperated cutting edge to it.

"OK! OK! To do that we'll have to call-in Fred, your CID colleague based upstream at Platts. You got your mobile handy?" Friender was also slightly maddened about the unwanted halt to any chance of swiftly identifying the murderer. Two good detectives and a wealth of clues surely had to be sufficient basis for nailing the killer!

But they were yet stumbling about still without that Ace clue. He had discovered no sign of any attempt to hide information vital to anybody investigating the murder. That would have made the task so much easier, because a clue as to why most times led to the vital clue as to who. This was truly proving to be a most exasperating case to solve!

Chapter 12

Once again with both feet, shod with heavy-duty waterproof trekkers, planted firmly on Platt's Ait Island at the end of the narrow bridge, Friender glanced quickly around probingly. He was now well-acquainted with the Ait and its derelict studios, having visited it previously several times in his quest for meaningful clues to finding the murderer. It pleased him that nothing much had changed because that allowed his brain to focus on finally solving the ever more urgent issue of how the murder had actually been performed. Years ago, his then wife had always tried to 'do' six things at once; the resultant chaos had motivated him to always *focus* solely on the job in hand.

What had the police missed? He knew they had sent quite a large team to scour the islands' inhabitants for the guilty party. How on earth was a private investigator on his own going to find the clue? At that moment a deep voice hailed him from behind, "Tom?"

The loan hunter turned to find DC Fred Timmon striding towards him. "Ah, Fred, really good to see you. I was just getting over the horror of researching this whole Ait once again!"

The Met detective looked at him with puzzlement. "Why? I mean why search the island when I've done it more than several times since being assigned up here?"

"I quite understand, DC. We've changed tactics to one of focusing on a search for vital clues that were for certain overlooked last time. It's the only way we can hope to make any headway in our hunt for the vital clue that's eluded us all. It's not what happened where anymore? We've chronicled that ad infinitum, but who perpetrated MP Clark's murder well away from the HoC. I'm now pretty sure that it was an act of vengeance and that the whole episode was designed to utterly confuse the police after the body was found, not out here but in the HoC Lobby." Friender waited for DC Timmon to respond, hoping it would be in affirmative mood.

"I can't comment since I wasn't part of either the original HoC investigation or the first one up the river, here. I've interviewed a lot of inhabitants in this area but no one came up with the vital answer you obviously crave." The DC raised both shoulders to accentuate his problem understanding the private investigator's logic.

Friender banished the detective's doubts. "We can win, Fred! If we both change our way of looking for leads as we scout round the ait one last time, we will find that clue. First, if the MP *was* murdered right here, where's the evidence? Second, if not, then where did the murderer tempt him down river?"

"There's plenty of islands between here and Westminster. You're a free agent, so you can go explore them for your vital clue!"

"But which ones are wooded, giving the camouflage a murderer would need to remain unseen?" Friender re-iterated his conviction of a well-planned attack on a probably innocent man.

"Look it up, you've got a PC! Better still, buy a pack of sandwiches and have yourself a picnic travelling by boat down-river visiting each isle. Make some notes while you're at it and I'll store them in the River Police's archives for future use."

"Thank you, Wise One! What, if any, new information d'you have for me? You were brimming with excitement when I rang." Friender proffered open hands towards the DC.

"Both of the women you wanted us to re-investigate have left the area, even though we found no basis for distrust. We have swept the area for any evidence missed the first time." The detective replied.

Friender chose his next words carefully, cautious not to alienate the DC but eager to glean any new useful information that might give him that vital step in his quest to finally solve the murder mystery. "Have you found any evidence of the MP running dealings or undercover businesses out here, hidden from Parliamentary watchdogs downstream? If he did, those could form the basis for black market rivalry, angry competitors and murder to get him 'off the scene'.

"You've a vivid imagination for an ex-cop! Up here, on a small island, very little filters from Westminster Palace. I believe most MPs are too damn busy with Parliament and constituency business to ever manage side-line businesses up-river. In my time with the Met I've not had many dealings with MPs dealing in dodgy businesses. There don't appear to be any clues inside Parliament either that MP Clark was into shady deals. I reckon you need to look elsewhere for his murderer."

Friender nodded his acceptance of the DC's analysis and continued his searching over the whole island territory for the answer. 'Leave no stone unturned' echoed inside his memory cells from his boy-scout training years, so long ago. The fundamental question still remained. Had the MP come out here, well away from Westminster, just to relax and enjoy his hobby of exploring the inland waterways or did Platt's Ait hold some hidden key to explain his murder? In addition, what might the boatmen of the Thames be keeping silent about? Could they have witnessed life-threatening acts inside their river working territory that they were refusing to divulge to the police, or to him?

"We've ascertained that MP Clark was murdered well outside the HoC and there are strong leads to the Thames as the actual venue. So why can't a strong police force, strengthened even more by us, determine *where* and by *whom*? I know from experience that we can solve the mystery but we have to find and use that vital clue."

"You and me know only too well from mutual PD experience that the Met sifts through thousands of pieces of evidence for every major crime it tackles. How beyond Jupiter are just the two of us going to uncover one extra clue that will solve the MP's death?" Timmon shook his head in disbelief.

"By turning the jigsaw upside-down and re-examining the circumstances of the case, under a fresh philosophy of detailed investigation Behind the Scenes. The question of Why? Needs to be pondered far more often. So, let's assume

I'm correct and together go back over the facts of the MP's last days: Not as your colleagues and others did before but from a new perspective, as if we'd never worked on the murder mystery before." The private detective raised both eyebrows high.

The DC paused before replying, as if questioning the investigator's rationale of suddenly changing tactics. "Why? We more or less agreed only minutes ago that we'd find no new clues on this island! We need to move on, which is why I said to hire a river boat and to explore the Aits downstream."

"Absolutely! Can you lay your hands on a River Police patrol launch?" Friender turned to stare at the river which never ceased to course past on its way towards the sea. Could he not borrow some of its urgency!

"I doubt it, not without higher authority!" the DC insisted.

"Just mention Superintendent Lacey; that should overcome difficulties in compliance with any request I make. He talked me into assisting the hunt for Clark's murderer, so holds the reins. I believe the HoC would willingly support any special needs to find the killer of their MP colleague." Friender's final remark was more of an observation than a concrete fact. Parliamentarians were currently renowned for indecision.

They set off in a River Patrol police launch from Westminster with the strong intention of quickly exploring each island on the way up-river. Westminster itself had been built long ago on Thorney Isle. They agreed with the skipper that it would be impossible to examine all the Aits in the Thames, but those down-river from the group of Tagg's, Garrick's, and Plaitt's were of significance as likely places for the murder of the MP to have taken place.

Exactly how he, Member of Parliament, had been enticed onto whichever Ait had been selected by the murderer remained a mystery; hopefully to be revealed later in the new murder investigation. Friender almost desperately hoped that the police could unearth new facts about the murder that would provide him with the vital clue he disparately sought.

Each of the river islands they investigated upstream from Steven's Eyot, Kingston on Thames, where the River Police launch started from, were wooded, although some possessed only minimal shrub covering. On these, the investigator concluded that there was not enough camouflage for the murder to have taken place. Friender noted in the summary report he had decided to keep for personal use that on none of these 'open' islands did any of the search party find the remotest evidence of a crime having been committed.

The frustration he felt growing inside his brain almost burnt the neurons with anger. How did one person murder an MP somewhere outside parliamentary buildings without leaving a single clue that the police and an investigator could find; just enough evidence to reveal the criminal perpetrator? The lethal act must have been planned ahead, right to the minutest detail of isolation of the victim and subsequent attack in the neck with a lethally penetrating dagger!

He reminded himself for the nth time that the chief inspector of police had merely asked him to find basic information that had been missed during the earlier investigation, not to attempt to solve the murder mystery himself! But he had pretty quickly become fascinated by the case; not least because it involved no less a person than an MP! Now hooked, he could not give up trying his hardest to find the criminal killer! He had never given up on a case in the past. So, why start now?

Was Platt's Ait going to keep on refusing to yield any secrets it held about a recent murder in the wooded terrain? The island had experienced a busy history since the mid-eighteenth century—mostly boat building, holiday trafficking and navy craft. But did it also have a history of death, either by misadventure or out and out murder? The chief inspector could find out for him, but why waste the officer's precious time? Friender had noticed that the police search launch missed out Tagg's Island and the smaller Ash Island, which was only yards upstream from Hampton Court Palace. That made the island a highly unlikely location for a murder, in full view from Hampton Court bridge across the Thames;

especially that of a MP! There were several larger islands downstream that could have been the site of murder.

But he, private investigator, just had to visit Ash island to satisfy his innate curiosity and, he hoped, allow him to remove it from his mental list of possible murder locations. Real detective slogs often required more elimination of possibilities than finding new positive leads.

"Ever visited Ash Island, Fred?"

"Never had any reason to! What d'you expect to find there, on such a small piece of wooded land, mid-river?"

"Clues! We know the MP wasn't murdered actually in the HoC, even though his dead body was found there weeks ago. I've deduced that he was killed up-river actually on the Thames—reckon it was much simpler to float the corpse downstream from an island to Westminster than to transport it overland by car? We need to find the necessary evidence on an island to back-up my theory. There are several islands down river passed Hampton Court towards Kingston and beyond but I'm betting on Ash, 'cos it's closer to Westminster and a really small ait; so unlikely to be of public interest."

The DC hesitated in his response. This investigator was private and had no authority over him; caution was a wise route to take. "You reckon it's vital for us to visit such a small island?"

"I do, for reasons I've already given. Shall we go?" Friender recognised he was coercing the detective without authority but his experience drove him to insist. He had not developed his reputation for solving mystery murder cases by 'abandoning the chase' just when his instincts began to develop a revised plan of investigation based on previously undiscovered new clues!

The River Police launch sped rapidly past other river craft on the Thames and in a short time Friender was stepping ashore on Ash Island. He felt unable to claim any excitement but did experience a sense that the murder investigation was at last evolving more positively towards a solution of who exactly had stabbed the MP to death. The why still remained an unknown but each step forward he achieved clarified the actual sequence of events involved in the murder mystery. He was going to win!

"I warned you there'd be nothing much here on such a secluded spot to lead us to the murderer!" DC Fred Timmon dismissed any slightest triumph Friender might have been feeling.

"Wrong, Fred; you haven't yet experienced "Why?" as the prime query to resolve at any potential crime scene you inspect. We've already elaborated on my rationale for coming here but now we are here our immediate task is to search every inch for any vital clues a murderer would leave behind. You're younger and fitter than me, so you take the ground level plus the first foot up and I'll cover the rest."

They set about the odd task as meticulously as Friender could instil in his police comrade. But after nearly one hour of searching there seemed to be nothing on the island they could uncover that might have interested the murdered MP enough to allow him to be enticed here. There were house boats moored on the river edge around the island, access to the Thames edge close to Hampton, evidence of boat building in days past, but no really major attraction.

The main reason for the dead MP exploring the Thames had apparently been the lock systems, originally installed by the predecessors of *British Waterways*, who now managed them. There was, of course, no major lock system on this tiny island! So what was he, private investigator, failing to link together the final stages of the murder, the organisation of a meeting on Ash and the act of stabbing in the neck to cause fatal blood loss? Who possessed the vital anatomical knowledge to execute an exact vertical severance of the jugular to cause almost instant fatal haemorrhage? He Must revisit his case-notes on all the suspects for details of their individual training and qualifications.

"Ahh!" the DC suddenly shouted out in excited voice. Bending over in the river water that lapped the island's shore closest to the Hampton Court Road, Timmon recovered a shiny disposable scalpel with razor sharp blade attached.

"Brilliant, Fred! That virtually seals the evidence for the MP's murder right here. Well done, well done! We can now assume I'm right, and the bonus is that we're able to narrow down the list of persons we know who could've enticed the MP here in order to kill him largely out of public sight."

"Male or female?", the DC frowned at the investigator. "Are you speculating for a work colleague in the House of Commons or jealousy on the part of one of the dozens upon dozens of women he's renowned for fancying and romancing with?"

"Speculation is not a framework for use by ace investigators, police or private. We need to get back to Westminster, Fred, to sift through all the data we've gathered on acquaintances of the MP; business or parliamentary or casual or otherwise. We've a solid character map to formulate which we can then use to identify the murderer *in person*. You can then lawfully arrest them; as I've not been slow to point out before. I reckon Ash Island has yielded any secrets it was holding, so let's press on Sherlock! I say, back to Westminster."

Friender's new mood of optimism instantly vaporised when he opened the door to his office. The room had been savagely attacked, or stormed to put it aptly. All his neatly sorted files about the murder case were strewn over every inch of the floor. His temporary desk had been turned upside down and the chair placed on top, also upside down.

Several large sheets of art paper were stuck to the walls with tape; each crudely decorated with violently malevolent and purposely threatening graffiti:

GO BACK TO *YOUR PIT* IN THE COUNTRY RATFACE;
GET LOST NOSE-ACHE; MIND YOUR OWN DAMN BUSINESS;
D'YOU WANT *YOUR* THROAT SLIT *TOO*?
WHAT'S DEAD IS DEAD, SO LEAVE IT TO ROT YOU SCUMBAG.
MIND YOUR BACK 24, 'COS WE'LL ATTACK YOU NEXT FOR SURE!
ASKING FOR A SLIT NECK ARE YOU?

Gory Red paint was smeared over many of the sheets to increase the savagery of the threats.

All this sudden unexpected, gory malice almost *inflicted* upon his workplace was enough to force Friender to feel an instant need to sit down; to stop his legs shaking and to relieve sudden pain in his senses. His brain was too disturbed by the gruesome atrocity to digest or even absorb-in all the chaotic happenings. However, in old but well-trained police ways he pulled out his mobile phone and exited the horrific threat scene into the corridor outside, to contact his police inspector for hasty vital advice.

"It's not an unusual scenario in the city these days, Tom. Violent remonstration of rage over attempts to govern or expose are not infrequent; even in higher strata of business such as that involving an MP." The DI's voice was calm and reassuring. "As you should recall, the big fear criminals suffer is to be exposed or 'found-out'. They'll even kill police officers to prevent it: desperate to maintain their anonymity."

Friedman felt left unsure as to what line of private investigation to follow. Should he admit his doubt, or pause long enough for his temporary boss to come up with a feasible solution?

"Judging from what DC Swift, Westminster has reported to me, you've already come up with your next avenue of enquiry." The DI's voice on Friender's mobile remained supportive.

"Please remind me?" The private investigator felt just a modicum of doubt about his own skills.

"To go back, rather than upward and onward, and re-examine all your data or clues on Clark's intimate colleagues in the HoC. We may well have underestimated the anger that lobbies both in and outside the House felt about actual legal protection of Wild Life. I've plenty of encounters with persons ardently vocal against new or revised legislature; especially any involving the environment." The DI guffawed wryly over the mobile.

"OK. It's going back a few weeks, but I indirectly recall speaking with four or five women and at least two men who were closely involved with the MP's personal and office affairs in the HoC." Friender replied. "I can't quite recall whether they were *for* or *against* Clark's ambition for better wildlife protection *in law*."

"I suggest you return to the HoC and find out; aim to refresh your memory! I'll arrange a new temporary office for you. Oh! As I said what seems weeks ago, make some progress Old-hand OR get out! Parliament's been waiting far too long for an answer from you! Westminster may be totally dishevelled at the moment, one could say 'at sixes and sevens', even after centuries in existence, but its members still won't wait for you to solve the murder *sometime!*"

"Thank you for your stern advice, Inspector; very supportive after my verbal assault in the temporary office! Yes, please, for a new office. In the meantime, I'll go back to the dead MP's place of work—better to work in a provisional morgue than being forced out on the street! I've an inkling of most likely culprit of the murder, so that gives me a starting point. I'll be in touch." Friender silenced his mobile phone.

Returning to the HoC gave no promise of quick answers but it did give him the warming sense of *coming home* just for a moment. The Entrance lobby seemed as enormously solid and lofty as ever and Friender felt the corridors radiating off it offered a greater personal sureness of progress about to be made. He made his way back to the no longer empty ex-MP's working quarters as swiftly as possible.

There down in the offices, he sensed real inspiration to re-find parliamentarians and secretaries he knew well. Experience had instilled in him that *Esprit de corps* could be vital in the task of final solution of complex murder mysteries. Their help could speed his solving of the case much quicker.

"Anyone found new leads to give us a clearer picture of what MP Clark was planning, or what any of his colleagues found so offensive that they were driven to murder him?" He looked around hopefully, although his gut feeling was far from expectant of any positive progress in the dilemma.

"There is some evidence that a Selene Teemore in parliament was very closely attached to Sir Peter Clark and assisted in his work with the proposed Wildlife Act before the murder."

"Yes, I vaguely recall her name. I think she so-to-speak entered the scene late in the MP's planning of the Bill?"

Friender felt real satisfaction at the disclosure—Progress! But was it enough? He could not dispel from memory his DI's admonition about the continued failure to unearth the murderer yet. And the HoC's refusal to accept any excuse for further delay was not going to vanish!

It was not so much 'Back to the drawing board, Tom' as 'Parliament wants MP Clark's killer revealed NOW'.

His still shocked mind re-imaged the almost violent graffiti stuck all over the walls of his now vacant office, just up the road from Westminster Bridge. He was no quitter but to be threatened so violently in what amounted to a Bloody Red Aura had sent shockwaves through his guts, mind, heart and all!

He sat down for a moment, to restore his mental balance. In the Met he had had team-mates or authority to lean on in any crises. Out in the challenging domain of sole operator, no such support existed. Yet, he did have team-mates around right now; so 'Get-on' he silently admonished himself.

"You OK?" a voice enquired.

"Yes, yes; sorry my attention lapsed. Has anyone else found clues about whether Clark's draft Bill had been tampered with, and-or the name of any antagonist?" he almost shouted. "Don't of course reply unless your evidence is brand new and was not discovered during the previous murder investigation by the police. Apologies for being repetitive but we are only chasing-up vital clues that never came to light previously." Friender softened his lower face into a befriending grin that he gestured head-wise around the office to all occupants.

"Where do we look now?" The face of the enquiring parliamentarian looked baffled.

"At all copies, and the attached notes, of presentations of the Wildlife protection Bill to the HoC. We're searching for false amendments made or added after each Presentation to the House or any official Amendment.

"How about a note in the margin specifying, 'excluding carnivores not officially approved and/or released into a park by Rangers'?" The enquiry came from a woman at the back of the office, just out of Friender's immediate view.

"Sounds like a prime example of the divergence of opinions over Clark's draft Bill. Keep searching folks—we might yet discover the identity of the MP's murderer! That elusive clue might just be close at hand," The private investigator nodded his head vigorously in encouragement of the find. He Was going to soldier on in spite of the full-hand of spades flaunted against him.

"Does anyone else have odd scribbles in the margin of any manuscript they're examining?"

After a flurry of re-examination of any documents opened for inspection, silence again enveloped the late MP's work station.

"Come to think, recognising my bad habits in keeping odd notes, are there scribblings on the Back of any pages you're examining?" Friender tried expanding the scope of the search for any clue whatever.

After further rustling of all the draft pages of the proposed Bill, nobody spoke. Friender felt real vexation at the impromptu team's failure to make any progress whatever in identifying a suspect murderer.

"Have you all turned your pages right over and studied every square inch of the back in detail? We can't afford at this late stage to miss any clue whatever!" His pursed lips and furrowed brow more than adequately projected his utter frustration. As an outsider, he could not question the DI's modus operandi in the original exhaustive investigation into the MP's murder; But he was surrounded by persons who might have all the answers, if only he could crack the unsolved question that hadn't yet been asked!

"'Watch Selene doesn't scupper evolution of the Bill! She's too keen to advance herself!' That's a quick note made in this notebook of Clark's. Any use as a clue?" One of the police detectives queried.

"Ta Alan, well spotted! I vaguely recall abandoning Selene as a real suspect early on after I was pulled into this murder hunt by the DI on grounds of her being too close to the MP and of her not demonstrating any vitriol whatever against him. Your discovery in no way eliminates her from the murderer suspects of course, but how can we reinstate her as the accused without some concrete evidence? Anybody got a clue they haven't spoken of yet or anyone got ideas on how to best proceed?"

The amateur gave way to all the professionals on hand. This time his query was immediately followed by strong discussions between persons in the office. Friender was gratified, because any progress towards solving the crime must rely on an exchange of ideas and opinions; a foundation for voicing that special clue he so ardently sought.

"Are we *looking back* too keenly, Tom? What if the murderer was actually, so to speak, Fresh on the scene? Might we all be skating past the vital clue you want because it's too recent?" One of the male parliamentarians raised his eyebrows high to emphasise his reservation.

"Yup, good point. Anybody else got ideas?" Friender felt a warm comradeship towards the questioner since his observation did open a new channel of enquiry. Where to next? he asked his mind.

"Assuming Clark followed the standard path for introduction of a new bill, that of consecutive readings in the House, Committee stage, Report Stage, Third Reading followed by a consideration of amendments, at which stage would a new-person entity have taken sufficient objections to the proposed Wildlife protection Bill to actually murder the MP?"

"What you're implying is that our murderer was upset far more by the MP himself than by the contents of the Bill he was drafting?" Another male parliamentarian had decided to join the discussion on cause for murder. "Hate is of course a multi-directional mental force that can strike from a variety of causes."

"Yes, it's a lot more dangerous than we generally recognise. But without the essential clue as to who hated the MP enough to actually murder him, we're no closer to a valid answer about who the murderer is!" A fashionably dressed but frustrated woman clasped her hands and pursed her vividly highlighted lips.

Friender reciprocated her frustration. The DI had called him in to solve the case, not to add more uncertainty about the identity of the killer! He had dispelled any case against the two most likely contenders he had originally identified in Westminster, also the two up-stream in the Thames around Platt's Eyot. That had framed his mental 2+2 final resolutions of who was innocent amongst his original short list of final suspects. Yet, he still needed to identify number 5, the actual villain in the equation, to solve his detective's enigma of 2+2mayB5.

"I share your exasperation at still being unable to identify the MP's murderer." Friender threw an 'I don't know!' look of exasperation at the woman. "Can we identify any person who began working in this office less than two months prior to the murder? Anyone here longer than two months is likely to have 'seen red' about the proposed new legislation further back in time. And anyone more recent wouldn't surely have had sufficient occasion to fully comprehend all ramifications of what Clark was trying to achieve, relating to Parks and Wild Life."

"It sounds a mighty complex problem to solve!" A younger occupant in the office observed.

Friender offered no response. His mind was remaining completely focussed on the paradox of the MP's murder but he refused to expand the boundaries of his thinking so late in the yet unresolved investigation. Shouldn't the police, of which there were two detectives present, take up any forward moves? He had no remit after all to find a murderer; only to furnish the DI with any new information he discovered. His gaze sought out DC Swift and DC Timmon in turn.

"Any proposals as to 'where next'? Can you and the HoC Guards uncover details of any recent additions to staff or any new parliamentarians who might have had some grievance against MP Clark? Oh! can I ask you to be wary of reinvestigating facts that the previous failed murder investigation did? If it's not new don't touch it could be a good axiom."

The two DC's responded with resolute looks; as if to say "Who the hell are you to be ordering police about?" However, they both bent quickly to the task of questioning the clerks about staff actions and movements.

Friender sensed a personal calming mental relief—he had absolutely no authority over Met officers any longer but someone had to inspire a new advance in the search for the murderer! Parliament could typically delay the progress of plans or Bills through the HoC but the finding and naming of any murderers of MPs must not be impeded in any way.

"I'm no skilled investigator anymore but do you two DCs think it timely to now draw up two lists, for and against MP Clark's proposed Bill, as revealed by all the answers given by persons in or using this office whom you've interrogated? That should narrow the spectrum of potential murderers, don't you think?"

Friender still felt reluctant to instruct expert DCs how to act in spite of his long experience as a chief inspector. It was Alan and Fred's job to unearth the most likely assassin, not his. He had to constantly bear in mind that the DI had requested a report on his new investigation, not a murderer on a plate! That prize was reserved for full-time police officers.

"Might seem a useful ploy to you, PI, but it could take days to assimilate all the data gathered into just a simple for and against!" DC Swift glanced at his colleague DC Timmon for confirmation that he agreed.

"Right on, Alan, apart from one small factor—I asked Pearl, MP Clark's senior assistant, to keep a close eye on any notes and comments jotted on any of the official documents we, as the investigating group, have written up to date. Using these sort-of additional surveillances, we've formatted a grouping of likely candidates for final scrutiny by you police. There's two males, close parliamentary associates of Clark's, and three females, all of whom are recognised members of the MP's clan of close lovers."

"Let's have your lists then, Tom, and be getting on with identifying the most likely criminal. As our seniors and you keep reminding us, Parliament waits not one minute longer for the murderer to be identified and locked up." DC Timmon's urgent voice well reflected the aura of anxiety to complete the murder investigation that pervaded the HoC office in which they were gathered.

DC Swift quickly voiced his proposal for the way forward. "Shall we first study in more detail the two males? Even in these days of equality, men are more likely to seek lethal revenge for business catastrophes than are females for sexual competition reasons."

"Hmm; not too sure that a jilted lover isn't just as threatening as a professional arch rival!" A seasoned parliamentarian voiced his opinion. Friender tended to agree, but knew he should remain entirely neutral at this point. The self-appointed team had narrowed down the suspects well but there remained a surfeit of unsolved questions, hindering identification of just who had intentionally cut the MP's jugular with a very sharp weapon. His investigative mind could not at this point resolve the million-dollar question. Yet, he remained convinced that the final exposure of *who* was now within his grasp. Amateur he might be but finding MP Clark's murderer he sensed was only 'millimetres' away!

Chapter 13

Or was it? Friender's conscience silently echoed that Long experience in detective work called out for extreme caution in 'counting unidentified demons' during the final lap of identifying a murderer. The 'colder' they were the more likely they'd have manipulated every event after the moment of taking life! Criminals spent infinitely more time covering their tracks *after* than planning and executing *before*. Often, an overwhelming anxiety to destroy the individual or entity that had so persistently upset the killer could trigger the act of murder, seemingly out of the blue to others.

"Have you, or the Met force, had opportunity to uncover the history and records of the two male chief suspects? Pearl, I believe one of them was in direct rivalry with Clark for pushing forward a new act in Parliament, at the time of his murder?"

"Correct, that was Carl. And not forgetting that a lot of parliamentarians and Bill planners contested MP Clark's use of the definition 'Wild Life' in contrast to 'free animals' housed within Wildlife parks, in his Draft Act! That expands the pool of potential murder suspects, don't you think?" The secretary raised her eyebrows.

DC Timmon quickly interjected. "I believe that aspect was dealt with pretty thoroughly by the Inspector at the time. I moot that fresh faces on the scene close to the MP's murder are likely to merit greater inspection for motive than persons who have long been associates of Sir Peter prior to his death."

"Agreed, Fred. You've come on the scene from a Scotland Yard MIT so must have some experience in murder investigations. Where next d'you reckon?" Friender gave way to authority in modern police detective work.

The DC pulled his DC colleague aside for a quick word before responding. "We've both come across similar murder cases under the DCI who selected you as advisor to this mystery. Least suspicion falls on the suspect last pulled in is a respected axiom in our division, simply because they've been investigated so briefly. The shorter the profile the less reliable any basis for suspicion."

"The team, that is all those present here in the HoC office, have scoured all the data available in Clark's notes and the draft of the proposed Bill for any significant clues. We'd like to hypothesise—sorry, but it's a better verb than *bet*!—that our criminal is either a very recent acquaintance of the MP or a person who's managed to remain in the background of Clark's affairs to now. In which case, we must re-examine details of all his advisers over recent years.

Silence fell once again in the office as 'The Team' devoted themselves yet again to step-by-step scrutiny of all the documents associated with the murder investigation; quietly but purposely watched by the two standing police detectives. The private investigator made himself busy to avoid close scrutiny or to draw any notice away from DCs Swift and Timmon. Theirs was the responsibility for solving the murder. He'd only been called in by the DI to assist.

"Judging by the current Mayor, the advisors undertake *all* the work to complete the tasks that their mayoral bosses intend, and promise the public to complete before the next election! If this is true of MP's also, should we be looking for conflict between Clark's team and that of the other MP who's been mentioned as a main rival for formatting and proposing new Bills?"

"That's Carl Letwing, who's current draft Bill proposes greater importation of wild flowers that are likely to become extinct in Eurasia. He's got as far as the Third Reading of the document, I understand." Clark's ex-secretary shrugged her shoulders.

"I appreciate your reluctance to take sides, so to speak. After all, what's the difference between the importance of conserving wild animals and that of saving wild flowers?" Friender also shrugged.

DC Swift instantly disagreed. "Both MPs would have felt deeply concerned about their particular business in parliament. And their teams would have strongly supported them, all the way, as they say."

"Hang on, Alan. Let's not begin disagreeing when our prime task is to expose and arrest the murderer," DC Timmon interjected. "I advocate that us three investigators each have a strong hunch that the offender is right here amongst the team, as you've labelled us."

"Agreed, Fred. But who here felt enough anger or hatred to actually take a scalpel knife to Clark's jugular?" The DC passed his right index finger up his neck to accentuate the lethal act.

Many of those present sharply closed their eyes in horror. "Relax folks, we're here to uncover who did it rather than play a horror fantasy! Does anyone feel we've reached an appropriate point in this investigation for them to end trying to escape detection and admit they're who we're searching for, the murderer?" DC Swift purposely scanned every person's eyes.

Friender mentally applauded the DC for his valiant attempt to 'close the case' but at the same time reminded his own conscience that that was the precise reason *he* had been brought in by their DI boss. Appealing for an admission of guilt was never going to succeed in this murder investigation! *The clue* had to be right here—but where? Thinking back, yet again, to his years in the Met, what had he experienced to be the prime source of conflict troubling all major participants in and around Parliament? *Ah! Failure in the eyes of either colleagues or members belonging to other parties.* So, *who* had Clark himself either despised or feared the most?

Was that person actually here in the office or was he or she, clever enough to remain *incognito*?

He sensed his brain almost resonating with the new task of shunting all the information he had amassed during his own investigation, together with new clues just revealed by others, along further neural pathways inside his cerebral hemispheres in a quest to instantly frame the most likely answer.

"What have we all failed to take into vital consideration, up to this point? I'll answer that myself, not to waste time. The absolute distinctive *inner* personality of each of our main characters. The public, that includes us, always sees or experiences MPs as *outward* personalities. We've not taken the vital step to analyse each suspect on our list *in depth*."

"We haven't had the time to dig into everybody's past mate, back to even what toys they played with in the bath! Whoever the murderer is, they would have formulated the plan only recently—give or take a month or so." The DC's voice was firm with certainty.

Friender's lips puckered, accentuating his conflict of opinion. One unsolved aspect of the MP's death bothered him profoundly. Why the enactment of such a complex charade to confuse the whole murder; as if the whole event had after all only been a game that went wrong? The persistent uncertainty over just *why* Clark had been robbed of his future certainly cloaked the jugular stabbing in classic anonymity! How the devil was he going to arrive at a valid answer? This murder, in true parliamentary style capped the biggest *unknown* in the repertoire of cases he had undertaken as a private investigator!

"Wait a minute!" Friender had experienced a spontaneous brainwave in his hemispheres. "Are we shooting-too-high? MPs interact with their constituents too, a major aspect of their being voted *in*. Did Clark let one of his followers down, over a matter important enough to them to experience toxic anger?" He once again shot a questioning stare at Pearl.

"I know no more than you," she replied sternly. "I only worked for Mr Clark as his secretarial assistant. That doesn't make me a psychoanalyst! What all his clients thought of him, I haven't the foggiest!"

"Very wise viewpoint, Miss. He must have had hundreds of contacts or acquaintances. That's what being an MP's all about."

"Anybody else got a bright inspiration as to what motivated the murderer?" The private investigator tried to convey optimism. An unenthusiastic team was unlikely to expose the vital clue. "Shall we break for one hour? Please go away in this HoC to seek a quiet place, and of course some refreshment. Come back here to the office with all the answers to the culprit in the bag!"

"Would you two PDs like to come with me for a resumé chat, mostly concerning the history of this horror story?"

A reasonable walk away from the dead MP's old office, along several corridors, Friender halted to sit down in a handy alcove with the two police detectives.

"Firstly, Alan and Fred, I owe you my apologies for assuming a role as leader of the pack! I do have the distinct advantage of having been *in* from early on after the Chief Inspector called in the case. You two suffer the disadvantage of me requesting your help much later in this secondary investigation."

"So exactly where does all this waffle of yours lead us in finding the MP's killer?" Timmon was obviously unimpressed, even although he admitted to himself that the task of finding and apprehending the perpetrator was after all his and Alan Swift's job.

"I realised, after we'd come back from Ash Island, that we've touched on MP Clark's original passion for protecting wild life so little that we've as good as dismissed that major aspect of the case as irrelevant!"

"You'd better remind us since Fred and I never visited that part of the MP's history, right mate?" The PD from up-river around Platt's Ait acknowledged his comrade's statement.

"OK!" Friender nodded. "So, be prepared for a bit of history on Clark's chief motive in Parliament. If you want more refreshment at any stage, please say so. The murdered MP had been intimately involved with a new Act, to immediately detain and where necessary punish any individual who knowingly harassed or injured a wild animal located inside one of the UK's parks."

"This Draft Act was hotly debated in both Houses because of the uncertain definition of 'Wild'. Many members had seen previews of the proposed wording in one of the drafts. They had voiced immensely strong opinions over the need for exact clarification of just exactly which animal occupants, of any officially registered within any park, were included."

"This is because not all creatures in any park would be included in the proposed new Act. This naturally upset many members of the public, and also included more than a few of the dead MP's close friends and associates." He paused for a few minutes to let the PDs mentally digest the new details of the case.

"In our research around the Thames islands and back here around Westminster, we found a general disinterest or a frank ignorance of the proposed Act." Swift responded. "That mitigates against the murder being a spontaneous act out in the bush."

"I think we're agreed it was very much premeditated." The retired CI remarked. "Enough of digressing back over my reflexions on motives for the MP's homicide, we've a killer to identify and trap and you two DCs are the experienced team to lead us over the final hurdles." Friender stepped back a few feet to allow the detectives to take the lead.

"There is clear evidence of antagonism between MP Clark's team who were promoting wildlife protection and that of his colleague MP promoting the saving of endangered plants on the planet. My research here in the HoC clearly identified that. The verbal battles to establish new legislation in Parliament are almost legendary, despite the judiciary body itself almost being established haphazardly by our earliest Kings centuries ago." PD Swift opened his hands to emphasise Westminster Hall's famous medieval beginnings.

"That doesn't solve Clark's murder!" Timmon interjected.

"Fair comment, but the scene of any murder usually reflects the modus operandi. To eliminate the MP in his own office when it's so busy and crowded as this 'ere, almost guarantees anonymity of the perpetrator!"

"Except, PD Timmon, that the crime never occurred here, if you remember? Clark was deliberately murdered on a Thames Isle and then dumped in the HoC here, just to utterly confuse the picture and to lead police as far astray as possible," Friender interposed.

"Well, thanks to two cleaner ladies, you Friender and countless hours of investigation by Met detectives, the real events are fairly clear! MP Clark was murdered by a parliamentarian he must have known well." PD Swift added.

Friender was pleased that the law had assumed responsibility for tidying up the remaining loose elements to the case. It was the as yet unidentified ultimate clue that everyone, bar one, still needed to uncover. That process had to be led by experts in the absence of a Sherlock Holmes. His acting DI had not been looking for such a renowned detective when he had invited him, merely ex-inspector Friender, to provide fresh input to the second police enquiry into the complex murder. He was here to add an investigative mind to the quest for a murderer; nothing more!

But, as in his previous efforts when called in by the Met, could he yet again unearth the actual villain of the murder drama? If he did, would the HoC express any gratitude? Doubtful, he surmised to himself. Yet, was there an undiscovered master clue written in Leona Black's not infrequent involvement in the now dead MP's hectic life schedule? She had cropped up in Clark's affairs often according to the office notes; admittedly most often as MP advisor. That had confused Friender until towards the end of his search for the missing clue.

Leona worked in the same office as the murdered MP's team, only because Clark and the MP for the Department for Rural Affairs, Carl Letwing shared the large office. In itself, that had apparently presented few problems. Until the recent changes in the HoC resulting from the recent General Election!

That had resulted in new MPs, changed departments and a fresh brigade of over-active bosses. Novel squads carried greater risks of inter-departmental rivalry. Friender could still recall intense animosity between rival groups or teams within the Met. 'Back to Now' his mental capacities insisted. He ticked himself off for straying at this crucial moment in his exposing of the guilty parliamentary worker.

All this rational analysis inside his cerebrum had taken no more than seconds, yet he still experienced reluctance as a mere PI, an outsider, to assume the authority to actually name Clark's murderer. He noted the hand inside her jacket pocket and sensed her tenseness just as he spoke. "Can the two PDs please stand by alert! I have surmised from all the events encompassing the MP's brutal stabbing that his killer is Leona Black."

Before he could expand on his blame, the accused had a knife in her hand and was moving swiftly and purposely towards him. In the next instant, almost unseen, the vice-strong grip of a trained police officer had stopped her dead. She screamed at both him and her accuser in a shrill squeal, "*He had no right to plot against my hero! Wild animals are NOT more important than endangered plants!*"

Friender felt unwinding relief that the suddenly maniacal parliamentary worker had violently but spot-on revealed her raison d'étre for getting rid of the opposition to passage of her Private Member's Bill through Parliament. He had no need to say *anything at all*. He could at last hand the now solved murder investigation over to Scotland Yard. He sat down sensing long-awaited investigator triumph!

THE END